SOLDIER BEAR

Text © 2008 Bibi Dumon Tak
Illustrations © 2008 Philip Hopman
English language translation © 2011 Laura Watkinson
Photographs © The Polish Institute and Sikorski Museumere, London

First published 2008 in Amsterdam, The Netherlands by
Em. Querido Uitgeverij B.V.

This paperback edition published 2013 in the United States of America by
Eerdmans Books for Young Readers,
an imprint of Wm. B. Eerdmans Publishing Co.
2140 Oak Industrial Dr. NE, Grand Rapids, Michigan 49505
P.O. Box 163, Cambridge CB3 9PU U.K.

www.eerdmans.com/youngreaders

Manufactured at Worzalla, Stevens Point, Wisconsin, USA,
in July 2013, third printing

13 14 15 16 17 18 19 20   9 8 7 6 5 4 3

Hardcover edition ISBN 978-0-8028-5375-2 (alk. paper)
Paperback edition ISBN 978-0-8028-5436-0 (pbk. alk. paper)

Library of Congress Cataloging-in-Publication Data

Dumon Tak, Bibi.
[Soldaat wojtek]
Soldier bear / by Bibi Dumon Tak; illustrated by Philip Hopman;
translated by Laura Watkinson.
p. cm.
Originally published: Soldaat wojtek. Amsterdam : Querido, c2008.
Summary: An orphaned Syrian brown bear cub is adopted by Polish soldiers during
World War II and serves for five years as their mischievous mascot in Iran and Italy.
Based on a true story.
1. World War, 1939-1945 — Poland — Juvenile fiction.
[1. World War, 1939-1945 — Poland — Fiction. 2. Brown bear — Fiction.
3. Bears — Fiction. 4. Soldiers — Fiction. 5. Mascots — Fiction.
6. Poland — History — 1918-1945 — Fiction. 7. Iran — History — Pahlavi dynasty,
1925-1979 — Fiction. 8. Italy — History — 1914-1945 — Fiction.]
I. Hopman, Philip, ill. II. Title.
PZ7.D893635Sol 2011
[Fic] — dc22
2011013963

The publication of this book has been made possible with the
financial support of the Dutch Foundation for Literature.

SOLDIER BEAR

Written by
Bibi Dumon Tak

Illustrated by Philip Hopman

Translated by Laura Watkinson

Eerdmans Books for Young Readers
Grand Rapids, Michigan • Cambridge, U.K.

1

The air rippled with heat. At that time of day, the army camp was like a ghost town. If you ventured out into the sun, it felt like you were about to burst into flames.

But even so, one creature still came out into the blazing heat, bumbling along the path between the parked trucks and stopping to sniff at every vehicle.

When the animal reached the water truck, it stood up and grabbed the faucet. Its paws scrabbled away, but the faucet was too tight. Not one drop of water dripped out.

The animal was a bear. And the bear had never been to this camp before. It was so much bigger than all the other camps he'd visited. This was the headquarters. The bear's master was taking a nap somewhere, and the sun was so hot that the bear was close to collapse.

He shambled past the tents, but didn't find his master. He breathed in the scents that were all part of life in an army camp, like the odor of oil and gasoline. And beer, cigarettes, and chicken. And leather wax, sweat, and explosives. And, of course, the smell of miles and miles of sand.

There was a new scent too — one he didn't recognize. So he headed off to explore: when you smell something good, you have to seize the chance. The bear followed his nose through the camp. He didn't even care that his nose was almost blistering in the sun, because when you're a bear, nothing is more important than a tasty snack.

He took a left and then a right, and then another left.

He waddled around the tents until he finally found what he was looking for. Then he stood up on his back legs and began a thorough investigation. The next thing he knew, a deafening scream was echoing around him.

Shocked, the bear fell back onto his haunches, put his paws over his eyes, and pretended he wasn't there. He stayed in that position until he heard his master's voice. Then he peeped out guiltily from behind his paws.

"You bad bear, what have you been up to now? And what on earth are all of those things doing on your head? What do you think you are? A clothesline?"

The bear put his paws back over his eyes and started rocking slowly backward and forward.

The unsuspecting bear had wandered into the women's quarters. He'd never seen women close up before, certainly not screaming ones, and he thought they were a bit scary.

"Does that bear belong to you?" one of the women shouted at the soldier who was standing beside the bear.

The soldier apologized about a hundred times, but the women didn't want to hear his apologies. They just wanted their underwear back.

The bear had at least ten pairs of undies on top of his head. One pair was hanging from his snout and he had a bra around his neck. The bear was perfectly happy. Everything smelled so lovely and sweet, like flowers, and it was all dripping with delicious water.

The screaming women were part of a Polish signals unit. They were in the army, like the men. When they realized the bear wasn't nearly as dangerous as he looked, they came a little closer.

"Now all of our things are stretched out of shape," one of the women soldiers complained.

"You'll just have to wash everything in really hot water," the soldier said. "It'll all shrink back to the right size." He started picking the pieces of laundry off the bear's head, one by one.

"Would you like me to wash them for you?" said another soldier, who'd come to join the first one.

"We can do that for ourselves," the woman said. She sounded a bit upset, but none of the women could help but laugh at the bear, who was rocking faster and faster, still holding his paws over his eyes. "Hello," she said to him, in a friendlier voice. "Aren't you a funny bear!"

"Nice to meet you," the second soldier said. "I'm Stanislav, that's Peter, my best friend and the bear's master. And the bear? Well, he's Private Voytek — and it's about time we started chaining him up."

2

World War II started when the Germans and the Russians went into Poland, the Germans from the left and the Russians from the right. They stopped exactly in the middle, where they drew a line.

"This half is ours now," the Germans said.

"And we'll take the other half," the Russians said.

Poor Poland! From that day on, the country as everyone knew it no longer existed. It was a divided country with a "peace border" running right through its heart. That was what the Germans called the new border. It was a funny kind of peace, though.

As for the Polish soldiers, they were rounded up and put into prison. If you lived on the left of the peace border, you ended up in a German prisoner-of-war camp. If, like Peter and Stanislav, you lived on the right of the peace border, then the Russians locked you up.

This dramatic event threw Europe into chaos. Germany invaded other countries and millions of people were forced to run away and leave their homes. People lied and killed and in the end no one knew who was their enemy and who was their friend. But Peter and Stanislav both promised, "We're friends and we won't abandon each other."

But even though they'd promised, they still got separated. One day, they were put to work in different Russian factories. Very occasionally Peter spoke to someone who had seen Stanislav and very occasionally Stanislav spoke to

Poland, September 1939

someone who knew Peter, so for two years all they knew was that at least the other one was still alive.

Then something unbelievable happened: an entire army of Germans invaded Russia.

"We thought you were our friends!" the Russians shouted at the Germans.

"Ha!" the Germans shouted back, "We're only friends with ourselves!"

The Russians let all of the Polish prisoners go free, including Peter and Stanislav. The Russians thought: if we're going to fight the Germans, we could use some help from the Polish soldiers. But most of the Polish soldiers didn't like that idea at all. They certainly wanted to fight the Germans, but not on the same side as the Russians, because they didn't trust the Russians for one minute. All of the

Polish prisoners did their best to escape and make their way to the border.

After weeks of walking, Peter finally reached the border between Russia and Iran. When he got there, the first words he heard were, "Tell me it's you!" Then he heard the voice again: "Please, please, tell me it's you."

Peter turned around and found himself looking into the eyes of a man who seemed to be more dead than alive. But somehow the ragged stranger's eyes looked familiar.

"Tell me it's you," the man repeated.

"Who? What do you mean?"

"Tell me your name is Peter Prendys."

"Yes, my name's Peter Prendys," Peter said, "but why do you want to know? Who are you?" And then Peter realized. It was Stanislav! With his sunken face and a six-month-old beard, he looked about eighty. Peter's jaw dropped and then he threw his arms around his old friend. "Of course it's me!" he cried. "It's me, Stanislav! Who else would it be?"

Stanislav just shook his head and kept slapping Peter on the back.

"You look like my granddad," Stanislav said. "But older."

"Have you taken a look at yourself recently?" Peter replied.

"Hmm, I think the last time was about two years ago."

Peter and Stanislav had escaped to Iran with hundreds of other Polish prisoners. It was the only border they could cross safely to get away from Russia. They couldn't go back to Poland, because it was crawling with Germans.

"So what do we do now?" Peter asked.

"Now? We fight," Stanislav said. He told Peter that he wanted to join the British, so he could help beat the

Germans and free Poland.

Peter thought about it for a moment and then said, "I'll come with you, on one condition."

"What's that?"

"That we stick together. We never get separated again."

"It's a deal," Stanislav said, and they shook on it.

Peter and Stanislav reported to a British army camp where there were lots of other Polish soldiers who had escaped.

"Everyone here looks like a skeleton," Stanislav whispered to Peter when they were waiting in line for food that first evening.

"They won't look like that for long," said the soldier in front of them.

"Why do you say that?" Stanislav asked.

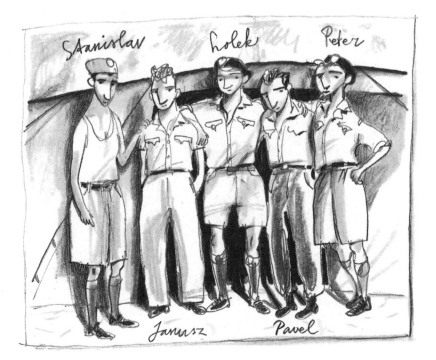

"Janusz takes such great care of everyone," the soldier said, nodding at the man who was dishing up the soup.

"Hmmm, I wonder if I could get a job as his assistant," Stanislav said, rubbing his hand over his empty stomach.

"No, he already has an assistant — Lolek. But if you behave yourself, I'll put in a good word for you."

That same evening, Peter and Stanislav got to know Janusz, who served the food, and Lolek, who helped him. Pavel, the soldier they'd met while they were waiting in line, introduced everyone. But none of them suspected that this was the beginning of a very special friendship.

3

The Polish soldiers completed a short course of military training in the British camp before they were put to work.

"Line up in groups of five," an officer ordered the group of over 120 soldiers one boiling hot afternoon. Peter, Stanislav, Pavel, Janusz, and Lolek hurried to stand together.

"You five!" the officer said to them. "Over by that truck. And you men," he said to the next line of soldiers, "stand beside that one." This went on for a while, until all of the soldiers had been assigned to a vehicle.

Then the officer gave them their first task: taking a truckload of equipment all the way across the desert to Palestine, where the British had set up a large army camp.

"No tagging along behind each other like a flock of sheep either," the officer said, "Keep your distance, or we'll be an easy target."

"A target? Who for?" Peter whispered.

"Something you wanted to say, Prendys?" the officer called.

"No, lieutenant," Peter said, nervously shaking his head.

"The enemy is everywhere, men," the officer continued, "so keep these piles of junk apart and only stop in sheltered places and when there are fellow soldiers nearby. The sergeants will be in charge during the journey. A sergeant will be assigned to each group of men."

And so they set off together: Peter, Stanislav, Pavel,

Janusz, and Lolek. Their truck was packed with sleeping cots, tents, barrels of oil, and boxes of artillery parts.

Their journey took them over steep mountain passes and along narrow roads. From early in the morning until late at night, all they saw was rocks, sand, and shimmering air. Sometimes, when they saw other army trucks parked up at the side of the road, they stopped driving. Then they could have a chat and nap safely while the others kept watch.

But one afternoon, Stanislav had had enough. He decided to stop the truck, even though there were no other trucks in sight for miles.

"That's it. I can't keep on bumping along in this oven," he said, jumping out of the truck.

"But it's way too dangerous here," Lolek said.

"Yeah? Well, cooking away in that tin box is dangerous too," Stanislav replied.

Janusz sighed and walked around to the back of the truck to open up their crate of food. They sat in the shade of the vehicle and took turns drinking from the water bottle.

Peter was just about to stretch out for an afternoon nap when he saw a young boy — that *was* just a young boy, wasn't it? — stepping out from behind a rock. He nudged Stanislav and pointed. Could it be an ambush? What was the boy doing out here in the middle of nowhere?

The boy slowly walked toward the soldiers. He was dragging something heavy in an old burlap sack. Lolek reached for his gun.

"Don't," Peter said sharply, and he beckoned the boy over.

Lolek whispered that there could be a bunch of bandits

hiding behind the rocks.

"Come on, scaredy cat," Stanislav said. "What do you think this is? Ali Baba and the Forty Thieves?"

"Hey you, come here," Peter called, but the boy hung back.

Stanislav waved a chunk of bread at him. When the boy saw the bread, his expression changed. He stood up straight and walked over to the soldiers. Then he snatched the bread from Stanislav's hand and stuffed it straight into his mouth, all in one bite.

"Look!" Lolek cried, pointing his finger at the sack.

"What is it now?" Stanislav said.

"That sack's m–m–moving."

Curious, Peter walked over to take a look at the sack.

"Don't!" Lolek called. "It's a trap." Peter didn't pay any attention to Lolek, but went ahead and opened the sack. They all held their breath, except for the little boy, who calmly carried on chewing his bread.

Peter just stared. "Whoa," was all he said. The soldiers leaped to their feet and ran over to see what was in the sack. Even Lolek came to look. They all turned in amazement to look at the boy.

"Does this belong to you?" Peter managed to say, using a combination of words and gestures.

The boy nodded. Two beady black eyes appeared over the top of the sack, blinking in the blazing sunlight. The eyes were surrounded by dull, pale brown fur. Peter didn't look back at the boy, but picked up the dusty little creature. It fit perfectly in his arms.

"A bear," Stanislav whispered. For just a moment, those brave, tough soldiers disappeared. Their voices became quiet and soft, and all they wanted to do was pet the bear cub.

"He's just like a teddy bear," Pavel said.

"A hairy little baby," Janusz said.

"I had a dog back home in Poland," Lolek said. "He looks just like my dog."

"Look at us! We're like a bunch of women," Stanislav said. They all gazed tenderly at the bear cub lying sleepily in Peter's arms.

The boy came over to the soldiers and pointed at the bread that was lying on the ground nearby. They could see how hungry he was. And they could also see that the little bear didn't have much more life left in him. Peter rocked the cub in his arms as though he'd been raising baby bears all his life, and Stanislav declared, "Okay, we're keeping the bear." And he opened negotiations, taking a penknife out of his pocket and handing it to the boy.

"But what about the sergeant?" Lolek said.

"Who cares about the sergeant?" Stanislav replied.

The boy left with Stanislav's penknife, a tin of corned beef, and some money. The bear stayed with the soldiers. Janusz held out a piece of bread in front of the bear's nose, but the cub hardly moved. Peter gently shook the bear and Stanislav tried to force the bread into its mouth, but it just closed its eyes and seemed to want to sleep.

Then Janusz slapped his forehead, ran to the truck and came back with a tin of milk and an empty vodka bottle. He filled the bottle with milk and handed it to Peter.

When the bear cub smelled the milk, it opened its eyes and drank down the whole bottle.

All of the soldiers started petting and stroking the bear cub again. They had no idea how it was going to work, but they all agreed on one thing: they weren't going to leave this little bear behind.

"We have to give him a name," Stanislav said.

"Let's call him Rover," Janusz said.

"Ali Baba," Pavel said, slapping his knee.

"Ha, ha," Lolek muttered.

"It has to be a Polish name," Stanislav said. "He's one of us."

"Voytek," said Peter, still rocking the bear cub to and fro. "It means 'smiling warrior.'"

All of the soldiers agreed that it was a good name. Stanislav poured some water over Voytek's head and said, "We hereby name you Voytek, little bear, and we bless you and pray that you have a long and happy life."

"Amen," Lolek added.

"Amen," repeated the others.

4

"What do we have here?" Sergeant Kowalski's voice sounded sterner than normal.

"Well, um . . ." Peter started.

"See, it's like this . . ." Pavel said.

"I told you, didn't I?" Lolek whispered.

"Shut up, Lol," Stanislav said.

"It's . . . a bear," Janusz said.

"I can see that for myself," the sergeant replied.

"Well, why did you ask . . ." Stanislav began, but he didn't get any further because Peter gave him a nudge.

"Sergeant," Peter said, springing to attention. "This bear is our new mascot."

"Where did you get it from?" asked the sergeant in a very serious voice.

Peter told him about the boy with the sack. He explained about the half-dead bear cub that had crawled out of the sack and said that the bear had been with them in the truck for two days and was already feeling much better. The cub drank milk from a vodka bottle and Pavel had made a rubber nozzle so that it was easier for the bear cub to drink.

The sergeant hunkered down and Voytek lumbered straight over to him. He lifted the little mascot onto his lap and stroked his head.

"Hey, please show a little respect for the 2nd Polish Corps," the sergeant said as Voytek started to bite the

buttons on his uniform.

Pavel told him the mother bear had probably been shot and the boy must have been planning to sell the bear to street musicians or a circus. "But luckily we got there first," he finished.

The others nodded and looked anxiously at the sergeant, but the sergeant had stopped listening long ago. He was looking only at Voytek and his eyes were starting to gleam. It hadn't taken long for the sergeant to fall in love with Voytek, just as the soldiers had when they saw the little bear for the first time.

"When we get to Palestine, the officer in charge of the camp there will have to decide," the sergeant finally said. He wished the soldiers a good journey and then he went back to his jeep and drove away.

The soldiers still had a long way to go. That evening they would reach the border with Iraq and then it would take them a few days to drive through Syria and Transjordan to Palestine.

Stanislav came up with one plan after another to convince the British commanding officer to allow them to keep Voytek as a mascot.

The journey of the Polish soldiers

"We'll bribe him," Stanislav said.

"Too obvious," Peter said.

"With whiskey then, not money."

"That's still just as obvious," Pavel replied.

"We'll build a really strong cage so Voytek won't be able to make a nuisance of himself."

"The poor bear. That's so sad," Lolek said.

"We'll teach him tricks, so he can entertain the C.O."

"That's even sadder," Janusz said.

"We'll clean the C.O.'s boots every night and sing the British national anthem three times a day, with all the verses."

"No, no, no," the others said.

As they drove along, there seemed to be no end to that unfriendly landscape. They lurched and jolted along the road and all that time Voytek sat on Peter's lap like a good bear. They sang songs, they gave him the bottle, and during the hottest part of the day they put him in a washtub full of water so he could cool down.

Voytek just kept on growing happier and stronger. His daily bath turned his dull fur a silky pale blond. He had his own handkerchief that he played with all the time; even when he fell asleep he clutched his handkerchief with his paws and pressed it to his nose. Anyone who saw the bear sleeping and hugging his handkerchief tight could forget that there was a war going on and that, elsewhere in the world, people were fighting and dying.

"I know what we need to do," Pavel suddenly said. "We just have to make sure Voytek's asleep when the C.O. calls for us to go and see him."

"And then?" Stanislav asked.

"Then he'll fall in love with Voytek, the way we did when we saw him the first time."

Everyone agreed it was a good idea. They had to be certain that the C.O. would melt and fall in love with Voytek, just as the sergeant had. But how were they going to get Voytek to fall asleep on command? And stay asleep?

"Alcohol," Stanislav declared, as they lurched over the three-hundred-and-eightieth bump of the day. The soldiers all flew up into the air and Voytek left Peter's lap for a moment.

"Alcohol?!" Peter exclaimed.

"But isn't alcohol bad for bears?" Lolek asked.

"Lol, stay out of this, okay?" Stanislav replied. "You can choose: this bear has a tiny little drop of vodka or we leave him behind in this boiling hot sandpit."

"Well, we do have a little vodka to spare," said Janusz,

who knew exactly what they had in the supply crates.

So they agreed that they'd give Voytek a bottle of milk with a splash of vodka just before the visit to the commanding officer. Then he'd be sleeping like a baby and the C.O. would let him stay.

Stanislav blew the truck's horn a few times to celebrate the plan. That woke Voytek up and, for the three-hundred-and-eighty-first time, they went over a bump and flew up into the air.

Late that afternoon, they reached Palestine. Soon the soldiers would be able to join their British allies.

Peter and Stanislav hadn't even put up their tents when Sergeant Kowalski appeared. He said the C.O. wanted to speak to them immediately.

"Can't it wait a while? Say, an hour or so?" Stanislav asked.

"Orders are orders," the sergeant said. "And make sure you take that bear with you."

Stanislav ran to Janusz and told him they needed to get the bottle ready right that instant. There wasn't a second to lose. Peter picked up Voytek, fetched his handkerchief from the truck, and grabbed the bottle from Janusz's hands the moment it was ready.

Voytek couldn't drink it quickly enough. His bottle was so tasty. By the time they reached the office, the bottle was completely empty.

"So . . ." the C.O. said when Peter and Stanislav were standing in front of his desk. "This is the hairy little soldier boy I've heard so much about."

Peter held on tight to Voytek and Stanislav tucked the handkerchief between the bear cub's paws.

"Well," the officer continued, "you men are aware that this is an army camp and not a zoo, aren't you?"

Peter and Stanislav kept quiet and looked down at their feet.

The officer came out from behind his desk and continued, "There's no harm in having dogs here, but I can't possibly allow a bear." He adjusted his glasses and took a closer look at Voytek.

Peter was having difficulty keeping him under control. Their little plan hadn't been entirely successful. Instead of lying there sleeping sweetly, with his handkerchief in his paws, Voytek had decided he was in the mood for a fight. He wanted to take a swipe at someone.

When the officer reached out to stroke Voytek, the little bear grabbed his hand in his front paws and sank his teeth into it.

"My, my," the officer said, "what a spirited little creature." He took a step back.

Peter was shocked. "I've never seen him do that

before," he said.

"No, no, I'm sure you haven't," the officer replied.

Voytek was now trying to wriggle out of Peter's arms and Stanislav had to keep bending down to pick up the handkerchief every time Voytek threw it onto the floor.

Peter and Stanislav were so embarrassed that they didn't know where to look. Like a couple of over-anxious mothers, they'd gone to so much trouble to make sure Voytek was on his best behavior. They were just glad the other soldiers weren't there to see it.

But then, against all expectations, it happened: the officer's expression softened. His stern frown disappeared and his eyes filled with tenderness.

"What a character," he said. "Such a will to survive." The way he was looking at Voytek, it was almost as though he was in love.

"We must enroll this bear officially as a new recruit in the Polish army," the commanding officer instructed a nearby corporal. Then he turned to Peter and Stanislav and said, "If we all showed as much spirit as this bear, we'd win the war in no time. Does he have a name?"

"Voytek," Peter whispered.

"Add him to the list of soldiers," the officer called to the corporal. "Private Voytek. You men, what are you waiting for? *Diiiis-missed!*"

Peter and Stanislav gave the best salute they could manage. They couldn't get out of the office fast enough. They had to run back to the others and tell them the good news.

By the time they got there, Voytek was snoring peacefully in Peter's arms.

"Well?" Janusz asked.

"Piece of cake," Stanislav answered.

"Thought as much," Janusz said.

"Right. Now I could do with a drink myself," Stanislav said.

"Oh . . . um . . ." Janusz replied.

"What do you mean, 'Oh'? You don't mean to say you used all of our vodka . . ."

"Um . . . yes . . . it all went into Voytek's bottle. Well, I had to make sure it would work, didn't I?"

5

The soldiers agreed that Voytek should sleep in Peter's tent in the camp in Palestine. It was Peter who had taken him out of the sack on that very first day in the desert. Peter had comforted him and cuddled him. Peter was the one who had given him milk, who protected him, and the one whose lap he sat on most often. Peter was more than a friend for Voytek. He was the bear cub's new mother.

Pavel found a metal washtub and put a blanket in it, and that was Voytek's bed. It was a perfect fit.

That night, Peter blew out the lamp in his tent, and a few minutes later he heard Voytek climbing out of his tub. The bear crept over to the bed, stuck his nose under the blankets, and then hopped into bed beside Peter. He only felt really safe when he was snuggled into that warm little cave. Voytek found Peter's hand, took it in his mouth, and fell asleep sucking on a couple of fingers.

Exactly the same thing happened every night for weeks. When Voytek no longer fit into his tub, Peter made a wooden box for him. He didn't sleep in that very often either. What Voytek liked best was to curl up next to Peter at night, just as he had with his mother when he was a newborn bear cub in the mountains of Iran.

During his first days at the camp, Voytek stayed close to Peter, but when he grew a little bigger, he started to explore a bit more. There was so much to discover. Voytek wandered from one tent to another to see what there was to see. That's how, one day, he happened upon the cookhouse.

The cook had the fright of his life when he saw Voytek. At first he thought it was a dog, but when he took a better look he realized that there was a bear cub standing in the middle of his kitchen. It must be the little bear he'd heard some of the other soldiers talking about.

Voytek pushed his nose up against the food cupboards and snuffled. He was starting to get a little tired of milk from the vodka bottle by now and he wanted something else for a change. His nose told him that there were large quantities of something else to be found here.

"Aha," said the cook. "I think I've just found myself a new enemy." He put his hands on his hips and stared at Voytek.

But Voytek didn't notice the cook. He was too busy trying to open the cupboard doors.

"Stop that!" the cook shouted angrily.

Startled, Voytek turned around, sat down, and looked at the cook. The cook saw those little black beady eyes, the woolly fur, and the friendliest face he'd seen for months.

"Okay," he said, "okay." He walked over to the shelf where he kept the fruit. He picked up a banana and gave it to Voytek.

"I must be crazy," he muttered to himself. "Now I'm never going to get rid of the beast."

In fact, there was only one resident of the big army camp who didn't want to be friends with Voytek — and that was Kaska.

When she saw him for the first time, she picked up a stone and threw it at his head. Right on target! She picked up another one. Another hit.

Voytek didn't understand what was happening and ran back to Peter as fast as his legs could carry him. He climbed up Peter's legs, took his hand, and started sucking his fingers.

Peter looked around and wondered what had scared Voytek so badly, but he couldn't see anything.

He was just about to put Voytek down when he spotted a movement on the roof of the shower block. It was Kaska. She had a stone in her hand.

Kaska was a monkey. She came from a zoo that some of the soldiers had visited. The director of the zoo had given her to them as a present. "To liven things up a bit when you're on the road," he had said. Well, she'd certainly done that.

Kaska was always coming up with new ways to drive everyone crazy. She stole chocolate from the soldiers' tents, or cookies, or shaving equipment, or jackets, or berets. She would turn the whole tent upside down until she found something she could have fun with.

Not only that, she annoyed the cook, threw things around, woke up the whole camp in the middle of the night with her screeching, and climbed into bed with the soldiers, leaving muddy handprints everywhere. Sometimes the soldiers tied her to a tree, but she always managed to escape somehow.

Kaska attacked Voytek more than once, too — and before long she was his greatest enemy. Whenever she saw Voytek pottering around the camp, she picked up a stone, a nut, or a handful of sand and threw it at his head. If Peter wasn't nearby to comfort him, Voytek put his paws over his eyes and pretended she wasn't there.

Kaska spent a lot of time riding around on Stalin's back. Stalin was a dog. He belonged to a British officer who had already headed off to the front, leaving his dog behind at the camp. Stalin was a big old softy and, since his master had left, he spent most of his time with Kaska. They went off together for little strolls around the camp. And every now and then, Kaska would jump down from Stalin's back, slip into a tent, take whatever she wanted, and dash back out to her four-legged getaway dog.

If any of the soldiers ran after her, waving their fists and shouting, she dug her little monkey heels into Stalin's sides and they shot away like a rocket.

To protect Voytek, Kaska was sent to the other side of the camp, but that was no good, because she just came riding back on Stalin. It was time for Voytek to find a play-mate of his own, so he'd always have a friend to keep him company and fight his battles with him.

"I think I know the perfect candidate," Pavel said one evening after yet another attack from Kaska. "Wait here." Ten minutes later, Pavel returned with a dog following him. It was a white dog with black spots, a dalmatian. It was just a little bigger than Voytek.

When the dalmatian saw Voytek, it walked over to him, and sniffed him curiously. Voytek hid behind Peter's legs, but the dalmatian didn't care.

"Go on," Peter said, pushing Voytek toward the dog. When their noses touched, the dalmatian started barking. Voytek was terrified. He dashed back behind Peter's legs.

"You coward!" Stanislav shouted at him. He took hold of Voytek and put him down in front of the dog. "As for you, you just keep your mouth shut for a moment," he warned the dog. The dalmatian lay down and started wagging his tail like mad.

Voytek looked in surprise at the swishing tail. What he really, really wanted to do was grab hold of it and put it in his mouth. He waited for a moment and then he pounced. The dalmatian was a bit too quick for him, but that just added to the fun. From then on, grab-the-tail was their favorite game.

"Ha," Stanislav said, "it was about time that bear learned how to entertain himself."

"But what happens when Voytek gets too big and crushes the dog with his paws?" Lolek asked.

Stanislav shook his head and said, "Not a problem, Lollie. By that time we'll have come up with another plan."

6

The dalmatian had no name. He must have had a name once, but his new owner, a British officer, hadn't bothered to ask what it was, so everyone usually just called him the dalmatian. Or Dottie.

Since they'd met, he and Voytek had become inseparable — which was just as well, because the soldiers had less and less time to horse around with Voytek.

Peter and his friends had been assigned to a transport company. They had to keep the food and water supplies stocked up and move tents and oil and sleeping cots. Later, when they got closer to the front, they had to drive trucks loaded with weapons and ammunition.

Voytek and the dalmatian spent all day romping around. They ran between the tents and whizzed about, chasing each other. Anyone who saw a whirling cloud of dust knew that the bear and the dog were up to their usual games.

Voytek grew and grew, until one day Stanislav said to Lolek, "That bear is twice the size he was, but he still can't catch the dalmatian's tail. Look at him!" Lolek shook his head and said that they were lucky that it hadn't turned out very differently, because bears were always wild animals — even when you thought you'd tamed them.

One morning, Peter and the others were eating their breakfast in the mess tent when they heard barking. And then they heard the cook yelling. The cook shouted at the dalmatian and told it to scram, but the dalmatian wasn't going to be chased away that easily. He just kept on barking and barking until Stanislav said, "Hey, where's Voytek?"

"In the cookhouse, I think," Peter replied.

The dalmatian would not stop barking. It sounded almost like a siren. Everyone stopped chewing and Stanislav said, "You know, I think old Dottie's trying to tell us something."

He stood up and walked over to the dalmatian. The dog dashed out of the tent and set off running. Peter got up too and he and Stanislav followed the dog to the entrance of the camp.

Peter asked the guard if he happened to have noticed a bear passing through, but the guard said that at that time of day he usually watched what was coming into the camp, not what was leaving.

Peter shaded his eyes with his hands and stared out into the desert.

"If Voytek really has run out into the desert, he's in trouble," Stanislav said.

"But why would he do that?" Peter asked.

"Who knows? Maybe he's had enough of the army and

wants to go back home," Stanislav replied.

They turned around and walked to the shower block. Maybe he was there, looking for water. Or perhaps he was with the British soldiers, begging a jam sandwich off them.

Wherever they went, the dalmatian followed them, barking all the time. Stanislav and Peter asked everyone if they'd seen Voytek, but no one had seen him that morning, not even the British soldiers.

Peter said that he wanted to go and take another look at the exit. "Maybe we'll see some sign of him," he said.

The dalmatian seemed to approve of that decision. He raced on ahead of the soldiers. When he reached the exit, he just kept on barking and running around in circles, chasing his own tail.

"Dottie, just stand still for a moment. You're making me dizzy," Stanislav said.

"There," Peter cried, pointing into the distance. Then Stanislav saw it too: right out on the edge of the world, there was a tiny dot — and it was moving.

Peter started running, but Stanislav called him back.

"He has at least half an hour's lead on you," he said. "How on earth do you think you're going to catch up with him? You'll drop dead in this heat!"

"But he'll be out of sight soon!" Peter replied.

Stanislav thought for a moment and then said, "You stay here. I'll be right back."

Two minutes later, Stanislav drove up in the water truck. Peter quickly climbed in.

"Come on, Dottie, what are you waiting for?" Stanislav shouted at the dalmatian. He held his door open so the dog could jump up onto the seat beside him and then he stepped on the gas.

"Why did you bring this slow old water truck," asked Peter, "instead of the jeep?"

"I have a plan. Just you wait and see," Stanislav said.

The heavy truck slowly struggled through the sand. The dalmatian bounced around every time they hit a bump, but he kept on wagging his tail as though his life depended on it.

"Hey, Dottie, you can turn off that windshield wiper now. I don't think it's rained here for a hundred years," Stanislav said to the dog, grabbing hold of its tail. "And you," he continued to Peter, "you look like you think it won't rain for the next century either. Don't worry. We'll catch up with the bear."

Peter stared at the tiny black dot in the distance. Voytek seemed to be going so much faster than they were.

"Come on, the bear's just gone off for a morning stroll," Stanislav said, to calm Peter down.

"You call that a stroll?" Peter said.

"Listen," Stanislav said, "we're in the middle of a war, half of the world is on fire, you don't even know if your house in Poland is still standing, or if your parents are still alive, and you're about to start blubbing because some old bear's gone out to explore. Wait until it gets really serious and the bullets are flying around our ears. Then you'll have something to worry about!"

The truck's engine squealed as Stanislav pushed it on through the sand toward the little dot in the distance. It felt like an eternity before the dot turned into a shape and the shape turned into a bear, a pale blond bear shambling ahead of them through the sand.

The dalmatian started to bark again and Peter called Voytek's name through the open window. Voytek stopped for a moment, looked over his shoulder, and then carried on bumbling along on his way.

Peter couldn't stand being in the slow old truck, so he threw open the door and jumped down onto the sand. The dalmatian followed him and they both ran over to Voytek. But Voytek was a bear on a mission.

"From now on, Voytek, you're going to wear a collar," Peter called to Voytek.

He knew that it wouldn't really help, though. The bear was so big by then that he wouldn't let anyone drag him anywhere he didn't want to go. Stanislav drove around in front of Voytek, stopped the truck and got out.

"Come on, old boy," Stanislav said, but Voytek just turned around and walked in the other direction.

"You see?" Peter called. "There's no way we're going to catch him."

"Oh, no?" Stanislav said. He walked around to the back of the truck and turned the water on full blast.

Voytek stopped short. He turned around on his back legs, lifted his nose in the air, and charged at the truck. With a growl, he dove into the stream of water and let it splash down onto his head. He lay there for a while. The dalmatian yapped and jumped around Voytek.

"Stan, you're a hero," Peter said. And then he said to

Voytek, "You are the stupidest bear I know. Who in the world goes out into the desert to look for water?"

"Two things," said Stanislav. "First, it's not me you should be thanking, but this dotty dog. And second, the bear isn't that stupid. All he did was head off for a little stroll around the backyard, and when he got a bit thirsty the water came straight to him in a truck. Am I right or am I right?"

Peter stroked the dalmatian. And with Voytek's fur dripping with water, the four of them climbed back into the truck. A big puddle formed in the cab, but nobody minded. It was going to be another boiling hot day, so it'd be dry within a couple of minutes at most.

7

"Blasted bear!" came a cry from the shower block. "Why don't we keep him chained up?" Stanislav kicked the wooden wall.

"Has he done it again?" shouted Pavel, who was waiting to take a shower.

"Yeah, you can put your soap away. We've run dry again," Stanislav said. "It's time Peter finally gave that animal some proper training."

Stanislav marched over to Peter's tent and told him that Voytek had gone through the entire water supply.

"Why are you telling me?" asked Peter, who had just gotten out of bed.

"Because that hairy bag of tricks belongs to you," Stanislav shouted angrily.

"Belongs to us," Peter corrected him.

"Oh, yeah? Who took him out of the sack?" Stanislav said.

"Me, but it was you who said we had to keep him."

"Yes, because he'd be dead by now if we hadn't."

"So he's yours too," Peter declared.

"But it's your bed he sleeps in."

"Okay, Stanislav, was there something you actually wanted to say?"

"What I wanted to say is that your pest of a bear has been up to his old tricks again this morning. He had a nice long shower and there's not a drop of water left for anyone else. Just thought you ought to know before you start thinking: Oh, I'll just go and have a lovely shower."

"Thanks for the warning, Stan," Peter said.

"You're welcome," Stanislav said, "but please, please make sure you finally get a good, strong chain for that bear. And use it!"

After his adventure in the desert, Voytek had done his best to find a more reliable source of water. The faucet on the truck was difficult to turn, but the shower was as easy as anything. All you had to do was pull the string and beautiful cool water came splashing down all over you. It had taken Voytek a day to figure it out and today was the third time he'd taken a lovely, long, and leisurely shower.

"Ah, there's the culprit now," Janusz said. Voytek came lumbering around the corner, calm as you like. His fur was still wet from his hours in the shower. He looked fresh and newly washed. When he saw his friends, he ran over to them and playfully butted his head against their stomachs.

"From now on, we're going to keep that shower block locked up," Peter said.

The transport soldiers soon received orders to drive their trucks over the border to Iraq. Iraq was oil country, and they needed a lot of oil for the battle against Germany. Without airplanes, trucks, and ships, they were nowhere.

Peter and his buddies were ordered to bring back hundreds of barrels of oil. So they packed up their things and set off on the journey.

Voytek sat cozily between Stanislav and Peter. The people in the villages they drove through couldn't believe their eyes. Voytek was no longer that little bear cub in a fur coat that was too big for him. He was as big as the other soldiers by now and his paws had razor-sharp claws that everyone was careful to avoid.

"He's as gentle as a lamb," Stanislav said to the British soldiers in the new army camp in Iraq where they were going to stay for a while. "The only things in any danger are the food cupboards and the showers."

The British soldiers thought Voytek was great. They spoiled him even more than the soldiers in the camp in Palestine. They gave Voytek as many apples and as much honey as he wanted. They even gave him beer. Voytek thought beer was wonderful.

"Not too much, eh?" Lolek warned them. "Or he'll go crazy."

"Crazy? And what'll happen then?" the British soldiers asked.

"He'll eat you up, guns and all," Stanislav said with a grin.

One morning, the men had some work to do in the camp store, arranging and stacking the barrels of oil. Voytek was bored stiff, because everyone was too busy to spend time with him.

It was such a hot day and he really wanted to take a shower. Not only was this new camp boiling hot, the wind picked up loads of sand and it clogged up his fur.

He headed off to the shower block, hoping that someone might have happened to leave the door open. When he got there, he saw that he was in luck! Voytek shambled over and pushed the door wide open with his nose.

Then he spotted a man in one of the cubicles. He was still dressed, which was strange. When the man saw

Voytek, he was so shocked that he started screaming and yelling. He fell onto the ground, put his hands together, and begged the bear for mercy.

"What's he done this time?" Peter wearily asked the two British soldiers who had come to have a word with him. Whenever he saw people approaching him with frowns on their faces, he always knew it had something to do with Voytek.

"You have to come with us to see the C.O.," they said.

"What's that bear done now?" Stanislav asked.

"No idea," one of the soldiers answered.

Peter hurried to the office, where the commanding officer was waiting for him.

"Go and fetch that bear of yours immediately," he ordered Peter. When Peter walked back a little later, leading Voytek on a rope, he was sure the bear's days were numbered.

"It's my fault," Peter whispered to Voytek. "I should have kept you chained up." He thought about the baby bear he'd pulled out of the sack a year ago, whom he'd looked after ever since, as if the bear were his own little brother. He stroked Voytek, who was happily bumbling along beside him, and said, "Do you know what? If we have to leave you behind, I'm going to stay with you."

Peter reported to the commanding officer, with his knees knocking. "Come in," the C.O. said, "and bring that bear with you."

Peter thought back to his first official discussion with the other C.O. at the camp in Palestine. He'd thought he was nervous back then, but this time he was really, really nervous.

"Don't look so worried," the C.O. said.

"It won't happen again. From now on, I'm going to keep him chained up," Peter said.

"It'll never happen again? If only that were true!" the C.O. replied.

"I give you my word of honor," Peter said firmly.

"Private Prendys, I honestly have no idea what you're talking about. I'd just like to borrow that bear of yours for a while."

Peter's jaw dropped. "Borrow him? What for?"

The C.O. told him that Voytek had found someone in the shower block who wasn't supposed to be there.

"A spy?" Peter asked.

"We don't know, because he won't talk. So I'd like to use your bear to see if we can make him a little more talkative. It shouldn't take any more than five minutes."

Peter handed Voytek's rope to the C.O., who looked a little nervous and said, "If you don't mind, Prendys . . . I'd . . . um . . . appreciate it if you could come along too."

Peter followed the C.O. to a building behind the office. Voytek lumbered along behind them. The C.O. led them into a small, dingy room and told them to sit down. A light bulb dangled from the ceiling and there was a table with two chairs, nothing else.

The door swung open and a man with handcuffs came in. As soon as he saw Voytek, he started shaking and sweating.

"Talk," the commanding officer shouted at the shaking man. "You can choose to tell us everything or you can become a tasty snack for our resident bear. He hasn't had anything to eat for a week, so I'm sure he's very keen to get started on you." And the C.O. pointed at Voytek, who was standing at attention on his back legs beside Peter, looking very fierce.

The man fell onto his knees and began talking.

He was indeed a spy. He had hidden away in the camp to make preparations for an attack and to see where the weapons were stored. He'd even drawn a map, so that the enemy would know exactly where everything was in the camp.

"And when is this attack planned for?" was the commanding officer's last question.

The man shook his head.

"When?" the C.O. asked again. He gave Peter a sign and he knew exactly what the commanding officer meant.

"So, are you going to answer?" the C.O. said, glowering at the spy. At that moment, Peter gave Voytek a little pinch. Voytek growled and bared his teeth.

"Tonight," the man gasped. "At midnight."

Less than ten minutes later, Voytek and Peter were back in the C.O.'s office. There'd be twice as many guards on duty that night. The C.O. gave Voytek two bottles of beer as a thank-you present.

"One for each paw," he said as he took them from his icebox. Voytek downed both bottles right away, one after the other, so the commanding officer gave him another reward: an afternoon of free showers.

And so, by the end of the day, there wasn't a trickle of water to be found anywhere in the camp. The only soldier who looked clean and cool when he turned up to dinner was Private Voytek. He didn't know what he'd done to deserve the special treatment, but as long as his friends were celebrating, Voytek was the happiest bear in the whole Middle East.

And the Polish soldiers didn't actually need a shower, because they were gleaming anyway — gleaming with pride.

8

"GRRROAH!" Voytek jumped to his feet and lashed out behind him with his paws. There would be no rest again today!

The soldiers and Voytek had returned from Iraq the evening before, bringing hundreds of barrels of oil and other important items.

"Hey, look, there's Dottie," Stanislav had said to Voytek when they arrived at the gate. The dalmatian was already waiting at the entrance to the Palestinian camp, as though he had sensed that his best friend was about to get home.

Voytek had climbed over Peter so he could reach his head as far as possible out of the window. He didn't realize that he was nearly crushing Peter, because all of his attention was focused on the excited dalmatian.

Iraq had been fun, but this camp in Palestine was the best place ever. In fact, there was only one bad thing about it: Kaska.

Voytek had just curled up for a nice afternoon nap in the shade of a palm tree when the little monkey leaped onto his head and tugged both of his ears. Voytek stood up with a growl and tried to grab Kaska, but she dashed up the palm tree, quick as lightning.

Stalin stood nearby, watching with a drowsy look on his face. He was like a faithful horse, waiting patiently for his mistress to finish her tormenting. But Voytek suddenly decided that he'd had quite enough of that monkey. Today was the day he was going to deal with her — once and for all.

He climbed up the tree after Kaska, but when he reached halfway, she started bombarding him with unripe, rock-hard dates. Voytek had to hang on with all four of his paws or he'd have fallen down onto the ground. He had no way to defend himself. The dates rattled down on his head. How did that monkey manage to hit him every single time?

But Voytek was so angry that he just carried on climbing, higher and higher. Kaska had jumped to another palm tree in the meantime and Voytek tried to follow her. The whole tree swayed dangerously and Voytek pretty soon realized that he was stuck.

The dalmatian spun around excitedly beneath the tree. It was a long time before anyone else noticed Voytek, though. Meanwhile, Kaska had scampered down the other tree and galloped away on Stalin's back.

"Oh, no, not again," Peter groaned when he saw another soldier approaching him with a frown on his face.

"He's stuck right up at the top of a palm tree," said the soldier who had discovered Voytek. Stanislav suggested that maybe there was a spy hiding up there in the tree, but Peter just sighed that the bear was driving him crazy.

The two of them made their way to Voytek's tree. It looked like a pretty dangerous situation. "Hey, stunt bear!" Stanislav shouted up the tree. "You comfortable up there?"

"Voytek, boy, just climb down! You can do it!" Peter said calmly. Janusz, Pavel, and Lolek came running over. They all started shouting up at Voytek, but Peter told them to keep quiet.

"Voytek," he called up softly. "Little Voytie! Come on,

boy. You can do it." Voytek looked down, but he didn't move.

"Let me try," Stanislav said. "I'll get him down." He spat into his hands, took a running start, and quickly climbed high up into the tree. Lolek shouted for Stanislav to come back down, otherwise both of them were going to tumble down out of the tree.

"Lolek, you're such a chicken! How else are we going to get that bear down?" Stanislav shouted back.

"Think I'll go and get an ax," Pavel said with a grin.

"Just hang on here," Janusz said. "I'll be back in a moment."

And, sure enough, Janusz soon returned with a British soldier. The two men were carrying an enormous can. When they reached the tree, they opened it up.

Peaches! Voytek's favorite!

Stanislav had already climbed back down by then, but Voytek was still swaying around at the top. He peered down to see what his friends were up to.

Janusz held up a delicious peach, dripping with syrup.

"See what we've got for you?" he called up the tree, waving the sweet peach around. Voytek's nose twitched.

"Just shift yourself into reverse," Stanislav shouted. Now everyone started calling up to Voytek again. Stanislav took a peach from the can, held it up into the air and then noisily ate it all up, smacking his lips. The British soldier told him that the peaches were actually the dessert for Christmas dinner the next day and that the idea wasn't for anyone to eat them now. They only had one can and there were lots of soldiers to feed.

"You said they were just for tempting him down, didn't you?" he said to Janusz. Janusz shrugged his shoulders.

Voytek watched Stanislav eating the peach. The scent

that wafted up to the top of the tree was so delicious that he couldn't stay up there any longer. Slowly, slowly, he inched his way backward down the tree. When he was safely on the ground, Janusz gave him the peach.

About thirty soldiers were standing around the tree by then, and they all clapped when they saw Voytek gulping down the peach in one bite and licking his lips. It was the most delicious thing he'd ever eaten, and he wanted more! He walked over to the soldier with the can and grabbed hold of him. He wrapped one front leg around the soldier's waist and plunged the other paw into the can of peaches.

"Our Christmas dinner, our Christmas dinner!" the soldier yelled. Voytek just managed to swipe another peach before Peter dragged him away from the trembling soldier.

"Tonight, bear, it's the chain for you, I swear!" Peter said to Voytek. Then he patted the soldier on the back and said, "Hey, come and have a beer with us this evening and we'll make it up to you." But everyone could tell from the nervous look on the soldier's face that he wasn't planning to spend any more time with Voytek and his friends.

Peter and the others went back to work and the soldier hurried back with his can to the tent where they were preparing the British Christmas celebrations. Voytek pretended he was off for another nap in the shade. But he was actually spying on the soldier with the peaches. As soon as the soldier had gone around the corner, Voytek slowly stood up and sneaked after him.

It wasn't difficult to work out which tent the can was in. Voytek's amazing sense of smell led him straight there. He stood nearby, watching soldiers busily arranging tables and chairs in front of the heavenly tent.

Voytek had all the information he needed. He turned around and went to look for his friend the dalmatian. And when he'd found him, the two of them casually slunk into the big cookhouse. The whole camp smelled so wonderful today!

"Oh, no, I don't think so!" the cook said when he saw his furry friends. "Can't stop to talk to you two right now." But Voytek and the dalmatian weren't interested in talking. They wanted food.

"Out of the way, you pair of greedy guts!" the cook said. "There's far too much to do. I have to roast a hundred chickens and peel a thousand potatoes." The cook really didn't need to tell Voytek that, because Voytek could smell it perfectly well for himself. And that was why he and his very best friend were sitting there, both drooling at all the delicious smells.

"Fine, you can have one chicken leg," the cook said, "and now get out of my kitchen."

When Peter headed back to his tent at the end of the afternoon, he was carrying a chain.

"Come here," he said to Voytek. Very, very slowly, Voytek shuffled over to him. Peter put the chain around Voytek's neck and then fixed it to a tree. Voytek sat up and gently rocked his head.

"Sorry," Peter said, "it's the only way." Voytek looked as though someone had given him a beating.

All of the soldiers who walked by stopped to look at Voytek.

"Poor little fellow," one of them said.

"Guess that's it for you today," said another.

"Bet he'll let you off the chain tomorrow," the next one said.

"Chin up, mate, we're all chained up here too. Only

our chains are invisible," yet another one said.

"Aw, it's such a shame," Stanislav said, "now there's no fun to be had, eh?"

When Peter went to bed that evening, he unchained Voytek. Instead of crawling in beside Peter, the bear quietly curled up in his box.

"Are you upset with me?" Peter said. But secretly he didn't mind, because the bear had been taking up a lot of room in bed lately.

Because of all that extra room, Peter slept very deeply and he didn't hear Voytek creeping out of his box in the middle of the night and slipping out under the tent flaps. The bear headed straight for the big tent where the soldier had left that delicious can.

He sneaked past the tables and chairs in front of the tent and wriggled inside. He snuffled around a bit and it didn't take him very long to find out where the can was: on one of the shelves at the back of the tent, where all the plates and glasses were stacked up in preparation for the British Christmas dinner.

Voytek shambled over, stood up on his hind legs, and grabbed hold of the can. But it was pitch black in the tent, and somehow he managed to grab the shelf too. The shelf fell onto the shelf below, which then fell onto the shelf below that. In a panic, Voytek ran back out of the tent, dragging two of the tent poles with him.

"Grab your weapons, men! It's an attack!" came the shouts from the surrounding tents. Within just a few seconds, they had surrounded the collapsed tent. The soldiers stood there, listening intently, weapons poised and ready to fire at the slightest provocation. But all they heard was the sound of slurping and munching.

"Oh, no," one of the British soldiers said, "it's that greedy bear again. There goes our dessert!"

They lowered their guns and went straight to Peter's tent.

"Prendys! Your bear's up to his usual tricks," one of them shouted through the tent flaps. Peter shot up, saw that Voytek's box was empty, and flew out of the tent.

Voytek had made a run for it in the meantime, up on his hind legs, holding the can with his front paws.

"Bring that can back here! Right now!" Peter yelled, as he ran after him. By then, the whole camp was awake and everyone was chasing after Voytek. Before long, there was nowhere he could run. But by the time they finally cornered him, there were just a couple of peaches left at the bottom of the can. Voytek was hugging it to his body. There was panic in his eyes, and his paws were dripping with sweet syrup.

"Let go!" Peter said. But Voytek didn't think much of that idea. He stared at Peter, stood up to his full height, picked up the can and held it to his muzzle. The last few peaches slid into the greedy bear's mouth. When the can was completely empty, he threw it away and slunk over to Peter, looking like a small boy who knows he's just been very naughty.

Peter stood with his hands on his hips, but he had no idea what to say to Voytek. He promised the British soldiers that he'd make it up to them. But how was he going to conjure up a can of peaches in the middle of the desert? Voytek nudged Peter's stomach with his head and held his paws over his eyes.

"Do you know what?" Janusz said to the British soldiers. "I'm sure we must be able to find some kind of tasty dessert for you in our supplies."

"You're not going to give away our pierogi, are you?" Stanislav said anxiously.

"I'll make some more for New Year's," Janusz replied. "Sweet ones and savory, using my mother's recipe."

The soldiers promised to help put the collapsed tent back up early the next morning. And when the British soldiers had calmed down, everyone went back to bed.

Before long, Peter heard a quiet little growl in his ear. He felt one furry leg slide beneath the covers, and then another one. Then he was gently pushed aside and, very slowly, Voytek slipped into bed beside him. Finally, he felt the bear's huge mouth latch onto his hand.

Still sucking Peter's fingers, Voytek snored away as Peter stared up at the roof of the tent, wide awake. What were they going to do with the bear? And what was going to happen when they went to the front?

Peter tried to think about other things, because he knew that your thoughts can really get out of control at night. They can run away with you and take you to some very scary places.

But it was already too late. Peter couldn't stop his thoughts now. He started thinking about home, about Poland. Did his parents have a Christmas tree in their house this year? Or was the war so bad that no one in Poland was celebrating Christmas? Was there much snow there now? Would there be enough wood for the kitchen stove?

Peter breathed in deeply. The whole tent smelled of peaches. He thought about his mother's pierogi. They were the best pierogi in the entire village. Would all of the children in their street still go to see her this year to have a taste?

How could he lie there listening to the crickets while in Poland the earth was groaning under the weight of all those bombs? What was he doing out here in the desert, while his country was being shot to pieces?

Peter took his hand out of Voytek's mouth and held it up against his face as he tried to chase away all of those awful thoughts. But the longer he stayed awake, the blacker his thoughts became. He started to wonder whether his street and his house were even there now. Would there be lights and candles in the village to celebrate Christmas, or would everything be pitch black?

Peter's heart started to beat faster when he thought about Poland, about his village, his street, his house, and, of course, his mother and father.

Were they safe at home?

He turned onto his right side and tried to forget about his gloomy thoughts. As he did so, he rolled closer to Voytek. Boom-boom, boom-boom, he heard, boom-boom, boom-boom. Under that thick, warm fur, a really big bear heart was slowly beating. He rested his head on Voytek's fur: boom-boom, boom-boom, the heart beat on. Peter closed his eyes and just listened. Life can be so strange, he thought, very strange indeed: tomorrow's Christmas and here I am, lying in a tent with a bear beside me and we're not that far from Bethlehem. And then, finally, he fell asleep.

9

The real war was still far away from Peter and his friends. Even so, the region wasn't safe. People weren't very happy with all those British and Polish soldiers driving through their country, telling them what to do and taking their oil. But in comparison with the front in Europe, it was a lot quieter.

However, that peace and quiet didn't last much longer. One evening, just after the New Year, the soldiers were given a new job.

"Men," the commanding officer shouted. "From now on, you won't be transporting barrels of oil and tents. You'll be transporting other soldiers." Peter quickly looked at Stanislav and could see that he didn't know what the C.O. meant either.

"The invasion in Europe has begun. The Americans and the British have already occupied part of Italy, but they're not making much progress. They need more soldiers there and you're the ones who are going to fetch them."

"Where from?" Peter whispered.

"Prendys, keep your mouth closed and your ears open!" the C.O. roared. "The men you are going to collect are spread all over the entire Middle East. You will be given a route so that you'll know exactly where to go. You'll fetch the soldiers and take them to Alexandria in Egypt, where ships are waiting to transport the troops across the sea to the front in Italy."

The C.O. paused before continuing. "And when you have collected all the men, you will also report to Alexandria for the crossing to Italy. Prepare yourselves for the front!"

A shiver ran through the lines of soldiers. The men from the transport company always knew that one day they too would come face to face with the Germans, but now it was really happening.

"They've come all the way from Britain," Stanislav said when they were back at their tent, "and took this great big long detour through Iran and Iraq just so they could go and fight to the death in Italy."

"Well, they can hardly march their troops straight across France and into Italy, can they?" Lolek replied. "They'd be goners."

"Yeah, I get that, but it's not exactly the easiest route," Stanislav replied. "And where do you think the Germans are getting all their soldiers from? They've kept Europe occupied for so long."

"I wonder if there are any Germans actually left in Germany," Pavel said.

"Does Germany even still exist as a country?" Stanislav said. "Those sauerkraut-crunchers are everywhere."

"Feels like this war is going to go on forever," Peter said

with a sigh. "It's 1944. We've been away from home for almost five years."

Any chance of peace and quiet was gone. The men from the transport company had to drive their trucks all over, through the sands of Lebanon, Syria, and Transjordan. They lurched, they slogged, they jolted, and they sweated, as they picked up all those soldiers as quickly as possible and dropped them off in Alexandria, the largest port in Egypt.

And Voytek sat there between Peter and Stanislav for all those weeks. He stared in fascination at all the new sights and he dashed off by himself whenever he had the chance to explore. He chased after goats, wrapped freshly washed underwear around his head, and begged for honey and water at every opportunity. And, to make matters worse, he learned to smoke.

"Hey, you might want to put those cigarettes away," Peter said to the British soldiers. But Peter smoked too and, whatever Peter did, Voytek liked to copy. But he didn't actually smoke the cigarettes. He ate them all up, the whole cigarettes, but only if they were lit. And if the cigarette wasn't lit, he'd ask someone for a light before shoving it into his mouth.

A few weeks later, when everyone and everything had

been taken to Alexandria, it was time for the men from the transport company to report for the crossing. They would not have to fight, but their task was, of course, to transport things. Not cots, soldiers, and tents this time, but mortars, shells, and grenades. Submachine guns, bullets, and cartridges. Bazookas, Sten guns, flamethrowers, and hundreds of parts for tanks. They had to pack their trucks with anything that could fire ammunition and drive it all the way to the heart of the fighting.

They knew it would be really dangerous in Italy. Even Stanislav the joker had become serious during their last journey through Egypt. They had been driving from the capital city of Cairo to the coast, wrapped up in their own thoughts.

"So, this is it, then," Stanislav said, breaking the silence. "Now things are really serious."

"Yep, it's do or die," Peter replied.

They stared out at the dusty road ahead and, without saying a word, they both knew they were thinking exactly the same thing: what was going to happen to the furry tub of lard sitting unsuspectingly between the two of them?

10

The dockside in Alexandria was swarming with soldiers. And all of the soldiers were carrying things.

Everything had to go on the boat to Italy: boxes of ammunition, barrels of oil, food, compasses, helmets, blankets, medication, extra uniforms, field telephones, back-packs, binoculars, jerrycans full of gasoline, flashlights — so much equipment!

The ship that Peter and the other soldiers were going on was already waiting at the port. Its name was written on the side in big white letters: BATORY.

Before they could head up the gangplank and onto the *Batory*, they had to report to the office, to the English corporal who was in charge of the passenger manifest. He gasped when he saw the big brown bear standing beside Private Peter Prendys.

"Is he supposed to be going on board as well?" the corporal asked.

"Yes, corporal," Peter answered.

"And I'm sure that one's coming too, eh?" the corporal said, pointing at Kaska, who was sitting on Lolek's shoulders. The corporal's eyes seemed to be looking in two directions at once, but his finger was definitely pointing at the monkey. "Yes, her too," Peter said. "And . . . um . . . they have a couple of friends."

The corporal stood up from his desk and went to inspect the line of extraordinary soldiers. He saw the cook's pot-bellied pigs. And the pigeons. And the parrot. Then there was the dalmatian, standing about halfway down the line and, right at the end, the size of a large calf, stood Stalin.

The corporal shook his head as he walked back to his desk. Then he said, "No, it's out of the question. It's against all the rules."

"But Corporal," Peter declared in a loud voice, "the entire crew has to come with us."

"Not likely," said the corporal, now safely back behind his wobbly wooden desk. "It's not hygienic and there's only space on the ship for men who can fight. A bear's not going to win the war for anyone."

"That bear," Peter calmly continued, "happens to be officially listed as a private in the 2nd Polish Corps."

"Don't make me laugh," replied the corporal.

Now Stanislav stepped forward. He was so angry that he leaned over the desk, ready to tell the corporal exactly what he thought of him, but fortunately Pavel and Janusz pulled him back by his belt just in time, and Peter was able to finish his story.

"These animals are our mascots," said Peter, ignoring Stanislav.

"Your mascots?" the corporal said with a nasty little smirk.

"Our mascots," Peter repeated calmly. "And our friends. They help to make the war easier to bear."

Now the corporal actually burst out laughing. "Easier to bear? Bear? Is that supposed to be some kind of joke? Hundreds, thousands of soldiers die every day and here you are, saying you want to keep your little pets. Easier to bear? What do you men know about war? The Middle East is a picnic compared with the battlefields of Europe. You men haven't seen anything yet!"

Furious, Stanislav came back to the desk, pushing Peter out of the way. "What's that cross-eyed English fool saying? What does he think he knows about us? We've been away from home for years. I could make a beach by the river in my village with the sand I've shaken from my boots. I'd like to crush that fat gut of his beneath the wheels of my truck." Stanislav spat out his words over the shaking desktop.

The English corporal didn't speak a word of Polish, but he was very interested in hearing what exactly Stanislav had said.

"Well . . ." Peter began.

"He was just saying," Pavel said, "that perhaps you don't appreciate just how much we've been through. And that he'd really like to tell you."

The corporal replied that he had no time for stories. Then he pushed back his chair and strode out of the office.

"What do you think the cross-eyed fool's going to do?" Stanislav said.

"Fetch a superior, I think," Peter answered.

Lolek told Stanislav to take it easy. And Stanislav said Lolek was a big old wimp. While they were waiting, Janusz took out some food for everyone from his kitbag, because the corporal was away for quite a while.

"A bit of food should help us calm down," he said.

"I am calm!" Stanislav yelled at him. Janusz shrugged his shoulders and said he certainly didn't look very calm.

Finally, the door swung open and an officer came into the room. He had stars on his shoulders and his buttons seemed to sparkle just a little bit more than the corporal's.

"So you want to take your friends on board, do you?" the officer said.

Peter stood to attention and said, "Yes, sir." The cross-eyed corporal came into the room and, without looking at the men, he sat down at his desk and studied the documents in front of him.

Stanislav asked in Polish if the cross-eyed fool could even read, but Lolek whispered to him to be quiet because they didn't know how many languages the officer spoke. Stanislav frowned, but kept quiet.

The officer looked at Voytek and Kaska, at the pigs, the pigeons, and the parrot, at the dalmatian, and then at the massive mutt right at the end of the line. He shook his head. "Why on earth would you want to take this traveling flea circus on board a military vessel?"

"Because they're mascots," said the cross-eyed corporal with a sigh.

"Did I ask you a question?" the officer said, flashing him an angry look. Then he looked back at Peter and listened as he began to tell him all about Voytek's acts of heroism.

Peter told the officer about Voytek catching a spy, about how he guarded all of the company's equipment, and about how attached he was to the other animals. He explained to the officer that the animals couldn't really live without one another and that the same was true for the soldiers. They needed their animal friends. He told him that the huge dog belonged to an English commanding officer, but he was already in Italy, and so was the dalmatian's owner, and that they'd both be very unhappy if their dogs were left behind in Egypt. And he said that the pigs weren't for eating, but for playing with, and that the parrot knew how to say, "Nazis, go home!"

Peter wanted to tell him even more, about how the animals cheered them all up and even comforted them at times, but he didn't manage to get that far, because Kaska grabbed Voytek's ear and twisted it all the way around. Voytek yelped and everyone gasped and Peter said it must be nerves, because Kaska didn't normally do that kind of thing.

Voytek didn't get angry though. He just covered his eyes with his great big paws and started rocking gently backward and forward. The officer shook his head, but Peter could see a hint of a grin on his face. He seized his chance and started stroking Voytek's ear, crooning at him, "Oh, my poor bear, poor little baby Voytie, come to Peter, yes, come to your Peter." Of course, that made Voytek feel even sorrier for himself and he rocked his head even more and lumbered over to Peter and hugged his legs. That big, strong bear was just a sad, little baby bear cub again.

"Just one moment," the officer barked. He left the office and took the cross-eyed corporal with him. It wasn't long before they came back this time. The officer was carrying a pile of papers and he was accompanied by a third man, who was obviously in charge. He not only had stars on his shoulders, he had a crown on his insignia as well.

"Men," he said, looking around at the chaotic scene in the office. "I wish you the very best of British luck. You have my blessing. Be sure to take good care of your mascots. And I wish you all a very safe journey." The soldiers saluted as he left the office.

The officer signed all of the papers and said to Peter, "You have my permission to report to the *Batory*, along with your mascots." Then he turned to the cross-eyed corporal, who was looking very annoyed, and said, "Don't just sit there. Put a stamp on each of these documents immediately." The officer gave Voytek one last tender smile and left the office, humming a little tune to himself.

11

Late that afternoon, February 13, 1944, an unusually colorful procession made its way up the gangplank of the *Batory*. It was an enormous ocean liner, which was now busy transporting Polish troops from Egypt to Italy. It was like a floating football field, but even bigger and with a few extra stories on top.

You might think there would have been enough space for everyone on a ship that size, but there were so many soldiers going to Italy, and all that equipment, and this time a small zoo as well.

"What do you think this is? Noah's ark?" said the captain, who was stunned to find all of those animals on his ship. But Peter waved the signed papers triumphantly and said that it had all been approved.

It took a while for all of the animals to settle in and find a place for themselves. The pigs stayed with the cook. The parrot found a home in cabin 306 and the pigeons moved into 307. The dogs went to the stern deck and Kaska was stowed away safely in the hold. But what were they going to do with Voytek?

"Tie him to the mast," the captain finally declared. And so Voytek ended up as the center of attention on that mighty Polish ocean liner. Everyone came to see him.

Everyone wanted to feed him. Everyone was happy to give up a cigarette for him or a bottle of beer. Peter had to keep a close eye on Voytek, because otherwise the bear might become a chain-smoker or a drunkard, or even worse: both.

Those first few days on board, Voytek had the time of his life. Peter was always nearby and the bear loved the fresh sea breeze blowing through his fur. He had great fun trying to catch seagulls, too — not that he ever actually managed to get one, but they swooped by so close to his head that he never gave up hope.

As Greece came into sight, an almighty storm blew up. The ship shuddered to the left and the right. At first, Voytek stood up on his hind legs to see what was going on,

but he soon felt so sick that all he could do was sit there and whimper and shake his head.

No one dared to go anywhere near him, because he just lashed out at anything that came close. Even the food that Peter brought for him ended up on the deck. In fact, Voytek was so furious with the storm that he tore his blankets to shreds.

When he realized that none of this was going to help, he slumped against the mast, covered his eyes with his paws and rocked backward and forward, as though he wanted to imitate the way the ship pitched and lunged over the waves.

Peter's voice couldn't comfort him and Stanislav wasn't

making any of his usual jokes because he was so sick himself that he spent all of his time hanging over the rail.

And if that weren't bad enough, it began to rain. Pretty soon, Voytek's fur looked like a big, wet, dripping mop. By the end of the morning, the only person on board who was still able to stay upright and walk cheerfully over the deck was the captain, who came to see how the miserable bear was doing.

"Hang in there, sea bear," he said, "there's good weather on the way." And no sooner had the captain spoken than the rocking of the boat began to slow down. An hour later, the sun broke through the clouds and Voytek took his paws from his eyes.

The bear was back! And how! He took a good look around and saw the mast that he'd been tied to for days. It was as if he was seeing it for the first time. He stared up and up and suddenly decided he was going to climb the mast. So up he went. And when he couldn't get any higher, he slid back down again. He enjoyed the game so much that he kept on doing it over and over again until Stanislav came and called him down.

"I thought I was going to die too," he whispered to Voytek. Voytek nudged his head against Stanislav's chest, so that Stanislav could scratch his neck. "We're going to war, old buddy," Stanislav said, so quietly that no one else could hear, "and I'm terrified. This ship is taking us straight to the shores of hell. What kind of idiot decides to sail to hell, eh? Don't most normal people want to head in the opposite direction? Oh, you don't understand, do you? Of course you don't, because there's nothing to understand. There's no sense to it, this whole rotten war, no sense at all."

Voytek sat down while Stanislav was talking to him and

looked at him with a puzzled expression. Usually, Stanislav gave him a friendly thump or, when Peter wasn't looking, a cigarette, or he joked around or wrestled with him. But this was different.

"That storm we just had?" Stanislav continued quietly, "it felt like it meant something, didn't it? There's a storm in Italy too, a huge one. Not a real one, but it's still a kind of storm. It's a storm of war. And it kills or injures everyone, and if we're not careful, it's going to blow us all away and we'll vanish, just as if we never existed."

Voytek gently held out his paws to Stanislav. Not because he wanted to comfort him, but because he wanted something to eat. So Stanislav took some chocolate from his pocket and gave it to Voytek.

"Don't tell Peter, okay? Don't let him know that I'm scared to leave the ship," Stanislav said to Voytek, who was munching away at the chocolate and smacking his lips.

"What are you whispering about?" Peter said, walking up and slapping Stanislav on the back.

"Nothing," Stanislav replied.

"Everything okay?"

"Yep, I feel right as rain now," Stanislav said with a grin. He lit up a cigarette as though he didn't have a care in the world. "Let's go get a beer."

But they never got around to having that beer, because a voice suddenly shouted, "Land ahoy!"

All the soldiers ran to starboard and saw that it was true: there was land in sight. They could see Italy rising up out of the water on the horizon, in the late afternoon light.

The soldiers started to dance. They threw their arms around one another's shoulders and sang, "Europe, Europe, we're here to rescue you! We're half crazy, but we're

to the front

not feeling blue!"

Stanislav sang and danced along with the rest of them. His face was white and his voice was hoarse. But they were all so excited that no one noticed.

And if you'd put your ear against the door of cabin number 306, you'd have heard another hoarse voice, the voice of the old parrot as it repeated, "Nazis, go home! Nazis, go home!"

12

"Hey! Move it!" Peter shouted to Voytek through the open window of the truck. He and Stanislav had just loaded up the ammunition and were about to make their first trip to the front. They were trying to drive out of the army camp, but there was someone in the way.

"Come on, you hairy monster!" Stanislav shouted, joining in. "Get your furry body out of the way. We're in a hurry."

Voytek ignored them and stayed exactly where he was: right in front of the bumper.

Peter put the truck into reverse, but Voytek wrapped his paws around the bumper and held on. When the truck moved, it dragged him along. Peter went backward for about fifteen feet, towing the bear all the way, but he had to stop because there was a tree in the way.

"We're not going anywhere," he said.

"We should have known," Stanislav sighed. He looked sternly at Voytek and said, "If you don't stop it, we're just going to have to drive right over you."

Voytek didn't move an inch. He rested his paws on the hood and looked straight into the cabin. Peter honked the horn, but Voytek had heard it so often that it didn't bother him.

"Just give him a little bump and he'll get out of the way," Stanislav said to Peter. "There's no way he can come with us."

"Are you sure?" Peter replied.

"What are you thinking? We don't know if we're ever going to come back," Stanislav said.

"Exactly," Peter replied.

"I mean," Stanislav continued, "that we could be blown to pieces on the way there."

"I know," Peter said.

Stanislav saw the expression on his friend's face. "You're not going to start crying, are you?" he said. And when Peter didn't answer, Stanislav shrugged and climbed down from the truck, held the door open for Voytek and said, "Make yourself comfortable, bear. You're in for an exciting ride to hell." Then he turned to Peter and said, "Just remember, this is your decision, so don't go saying I didn't warn you."

Voytek took his paws off the hood and quickly scrambled up into his usual place between his two friends.

"Hey, bear, it might be fun now," Stanislav said, "but you'll change your tune pretty quickly."

Then Lolek came running over. "What on earth are you doing?" he said "Leave the bear here! You can't take him with you." But Stanislav just shouted that Lolek should mind his own business, because he and Peter knew what was best for the bear.

"Yes, but you're going to the front," Lolek called back.

"Very observant of you, Lollie, and Voytek's coming too. You're either a soldier or you're not. You make sure that everything's tidy when we get back this evening. *If* we get back this evening, that is." Stanislav threw his cigarette out of the window and turned to Peter. "Let's get this rust bucket on the road," he said.

"Thanks," Peter said to Stanislav.

"Hey, you're welcome," Stanislav replied. "As long as

you make sure nothing happens to that bear, it's fine by me."

"If you want to keep him safe, maybe you should start by not throwing your lit cigarettes out of the window, considering the loads we're carrying these days."

"Those little fireworks back there? Okay, okay, don't panic," Stanislav said, lighting up another cigarette. He passed it to Peter, but Voytek snatched it from his hands and stuffed it into his mouth.

"What a bear," Stanislav said. "What a bear."

It was winter in Italy and the rain just kept on pouring down. The twisting roads were slippery with mud. Peter had to drive very carefully so that they didn't go sliding off the road. Progress was very slow indeed.

After an hour's driving, when they were still only halfway there, Peter and Stanislav heard a loud droning noise. It was in the distance, but getting closer by the second.

"Oh, no," Peter said, "German bombers."

"Just keep on driving," Stanislav replied.

They didn't say anything to each other for a while. Peter concentrated on the road and Stanislav held onto Voytek's fur and secretly gave the bear a hug.

The first boom came from nearby. The ground shook and Voytek tried to dive onto Peter's lap.

The truck swerved and Stanislav just managed to pull Voytek back in time, as Peter slammed on the brake. Voytek had almost clambered onto Peter's lap by the time the truck came to a stop in the middle of the road. Then there was a second boom. Voytek whimpered and hid his head in his paws.

"We have to find somewhere to hide, Stan," Peter said.

"I warned you," Stanislav replied. He pulled Voytek away from Peter, so that they could drive on and look for a place to hide. Peter soon found a little road overhung with trees, where the bombers wouldn't be able to see them. When the truck stopped, Voytek made straight for Peter's lap.

"Don't let Voytek see you're scared," Peter said to Stanislav, "or he'll panic even more."

"Scared? Me? I'm not scared," Stanislav said.

"Of course you're not. Neither am I."

"This is a good hiding place, isn't it?" Stanislav said.

"Yeah. Don't worry. No one can see us here. Hey, can I have one of your cigarettes?" Stanislav handed Peter a cigarette and lit one for himself. The smoke curled up out of the window and the rain rattled down on the truck.

"This is just the beginning," Peter said. He inhaled deeply.

"You're telling me."

Stanislav was holding his cigarette a little too far out of the window and it went out. He tried to light it again, but it was too wet. He took out another cigarette and gave the wet one to Voytek.

Peter said that cigarettes weren't good for Voytek. Stanislav told Peter to stop complaining, because it wasn't as if one cigarette really mattered right now. And as they carried on bickering, the drone of the airplanes faded away and Voytek sat up again.

"Do you think we're safe to go now?" Stanislav said.

"Let's get this show on the road," Peter replied, firing up the engine.

The closer they came to the front, the more soldiers they

saw. They heard the rattling of a machine gun in the distance and the occasional explosion. Up in the Italian hills, men were fighting for their lives. The Germans weren't just going to give up. They intended to hold on to the capital city of Rome, no matter what the cost, so they pulled in soldiers from all over to give them a bigger army to defend Italy.

Wherever Peter and Stanislav looked, there were wrecks of jeeps abandoned by the side of the road. They saw tanks half-buried in the mud and drove past villages that had burned to the ground and farmhouses that had been flattened.

"It's like a nightmare. A really bad one," Peter said.

"But this dream's only too real," Stanislav replied, staring out of the window with a stunned look on his face.

They heard honking behind them. An ambulance wanted to come past. Peter pulled the truck over and the ambulance raced by.

"Remember that cross-eyed corporal at the port in Alexandria?" Stanislav said. "The one who said we hadn't seen anything yet?"

"Yeah. Maybe he was right," Peter nodded.

The big army camp close to the front was a complete quagmire. Peter plowed through the mud and parked up next to the other trucks. It wasn't long before their friends Lolek, Janusz, and Pavel arrived safely in their truck. They were all so pleased to see one another.

Voytek poked around among the trucks as though he was at home. Lots of surprised American soldiers came over to ask what the bear's name was and if he could have a cookie. And Stanislav replied that he certainly could have a cookie, but that he'd probably prefer a smoke or a drink.

Then they got down to unloading the trucks.

The men of the 22nd Company of the 2nd Polish Corps lined up the trucks in a long chain, all the way to the store. They passed the heavy ammunition down the line. Voytek stood watching everything from a distance for a while and then ran over to Peter and Stanislav and took up position between them in the line.

"What's that bear up to now?" Stanislav said with a sigh.

"Oh, no. I think he wants to help," Peter said.

"No chance," Stanislav replied. "I can accept him coming with us, but we can't let him carry this stuff. If he drops anything, he'll blow us sky high."

Peter looked at Stanislav in surprise.

"What's up with you?" he asked. "Ever since we got to Italy, you haven't been your usual cheerful self."

Stanislav shrugged.

"You're not scared, are you?" Peter continued.

"Of course not," Stanislav said. "Just keep on passing those shells."

Peter looked thoughtfully at Stanislav, but not for too long, because the next shell was already coming down the line. Peter took it from his neighbor and carried it over to Voytek. Voytek then took it from Peter and waddled over to Stanislav. And Stanislav just took it and shook his head and passed it on to Pavel, who gave it to Janusz, who gave it to Lolek, and so on and so on.

Everything was going fine until suddenly a buzz ran down the line. A group of men walked over, with a senior officer in the middle. Every man who wasn't holding an artillery shell jumped to attention. The officer saluted the soldiers, but then he suddenly froze.

His jaw dropped and his face went white. This senior officer was in fact the commander of the battalion. But, for just one moment, he forgot all his rank insignia and decorations, his discipline and level-headedness, because, standing there, right in front of him, was a great big bear, well over six feet tall. And the bear was holding a huge explosive device in its paws.

"What is the meaning of this?" he yelled.

All of the soldiers froze on the spot. Not even Stanislav and Peter knew what to say.

"Well? I'm waiting for an explanation!" the commander roared.

Another deathly silence.

"Well?"

Lolek took a step forward. "Sir," he began, "we understand your concern, but I assure you that this bear is tame. He's officially listed as a private with the 2nd Polish Corps. He received his training in the Middle East and he's a valued and experienced member of our transport company. You certainly don't have anything to fear from him and, given the look on your face, we hope he doesn't have anything to fear from you."

When he'd finished speaking, Lolek took a step back. For a moment, the only sound was the rattling of machine guns on the front.

Then the commander cleared his throat and announced that there was no way he could permit such irresponsible behavior.

"I understand that, sir," Lolek said, taking a step forward, "but we need all of the strength we can get right now, whether it's manpower or bearpower. I swear to you that this bear is harmless. I give you my word. The bear always acts in accordance with military regulations. His name is Voytek."

The men at the end of the line had no idea that there was a hold-up, so the shells started to pile up halfway along the line. And because Voytek didn't see any reason to stop working, he simply walked over to Stanislav, cool as a cucumber, and delivered his next load, and then headed off to fetch another one, which meant that Stanislav had no choice but to get back to work too.

No one was paying attention to the commander now, who was just staring in amazement at the bear. And when he saw how carefully the bear carried the explosives, a little smile appeared on his face. But it was a smile that no one saw, because everyone was concentrating so hard on their dangerous task. If just one link in the chain gave way, the whole battalion could be lost.

Voytek's reputation was growing: he was the bear who carried artillery shells.

13

The Germans were hiding out in the mountains. No one could beat them in that tough, rocky terrain. The liberators were fighting as hard as they could, but they weren't making any progress.

It was raining and raining, the roads had turned into rivers of mud, and all of the tents were soaked through. Even though it was spring in southern Italy, it still felt very cold.

Every day, more bombs came falling from the sky. If there was a hit, ambulances came tearing down the road. If there was a miss, an ominous silence hung in the air.

The men from the transport company carried on taking new loads to their fellow soldiers on the front line, day in, day out. The army needed more ammunition, more oil and gasoline, and all sorts of equipment. The men also had to transport new soldiers to replace the dead and the wounded.

When Voytek wasn't helping them unload, he sat in his favorite tree. He could stare out over the bomb-scarred landscape for hours.

Sometimes he'd swing on a branch or dig up bushes and tear them to pieces.

"It's such a waste of all that energy," Stanislav said to Voytek one day. "You should take it out on a German."

"Or on Kaska," Janusz said. "She made a huge mess in

the supply store again last night."

"It's not Kaska's fault," Lolek said. "You know what her problem is? She needs a man."

Everyone looked at him in surprise.

"A man?" Peter said.

Lolek just shrugged and hoisted another box of bullets up onto his shoulder and carried it to the stores.

And that's what happened every day: lifting, driving, lifting, driving. They were so busy that they couldn't keep an eye on Voytek. He just did whatever he felt like doing — until one day yet another soldier came over to them with a worried look on his face.

"Oh, no," Peter said.

"That bear belongs to you, doesn't it?" asked the American soldier.

"Here we go again," Stanislav said.

Anxiously, Peter and Stanislav climbed into the jeep with the soldier. They drove down a mountain track until they could go no farther. There was a huge line of American army vehicles, as far as the eye could see. The soldier drove past the trucks, blowing his horn. "See this?" he said. "It's all that bear's fault!"

A tall crane stood at the bottom of the slope. Hundreds of soldiers were crowded around it, all looking up.

"Oh, no," Peter and Stanislav said, both at the same time. Voytek was sliding down the crane as though it were a playground slide. The soldiers were clapping and cheering him on. Voytek looked down at the crowd beneath him and Peter could see from his happy face that he was having a wonderful time up there on the crane.

When the applause died down, Voytek climbed all the

way back up to the top of the crane and carried on with the show. He'd never had such a big audience before. He dangled down from the arm of the crane and swung in the air, holding on with his two front paws. That earned him an even bigger round of applause.

By then, the military police had arrived and were blowing their whistles, but that just made Voytek even more excited. To Peter and Stanislav's horror, Voytek decided to take his act up a notch and he let go with one paw. He looked like a lonely leaf fluttering on a bare tree. The applause grew louder and louder.

"If he falls, he's going to make a huge crater in the ground," Stanislav said. Peter couldn't even speak; he just nodded.

The police came over to them and asked them what they were going to do about the furry circus performer.

"Well, to start with, the soldiers need to stop cheering," Peter said.

"Any better suggestions?" asked one of the policemen.

"If they stop cheering, the bear won't think it's so much fun and he'll come back down by himself," Stanislav replied.

But no matter what the police did, no one stopped cheering. Finally, after all the misery the soldiers had been through, they were having some fun for a change.

Peter climbed up onto the roof of one of the trucks and shouted at Voytek to come down immediately. But the other soldiers yelled at him to carry on. "Encore!" they called up to Voytek. "Again! Again!"

Voytek pulled himself back up onto the crane and started his next trick. He lay down on his back on the jib, the section at the very top of the crane, looking as relaxed as anything. Again, the applause was deafening.

"What's he going to do for an encore? A headstand?" Peter yelled at Stanislav. He'd been doing a lot of headstands recently. It had taken a great deal of patience and plenty of bottles of beer, but Pavel and Stanislav had managed to teach him the trick.

The military police were staring up at the bear too, with open mouths. Stanislav said he was off to look for some beer, because there was no other way to get the bear back down.

By the time Stanislav had found some beer and climbed up onto the truck beside Peter, Voytek was shambling along the jib to the pulley. The audience was absolutely silent. All of the soldiers held their breath.

Stanislav took advantage of the silence. "Voytek!" he shouted. "How about a beer?"

Voytek recognized Stanislav's voice. He didn't hesitate for a second, but put his head down and kicked up his rear legs.

"Oh, no!" Peter gasped. And before anyone knew what was happening, Voytek was standing there upside down, on the very tip of the crane jib, waving his back legs in the air. The crowd went wild.

Then Voytek rounded off his show by sliding backward down the crane on his belly and accepting his beer to loud applause.

"From now on, that bear's going on the chain," Peter said to Stanislav when they were on the way back in the truck.

"Yeah, yeah," Stanislav said, as he tickled Voytek's tummy. "Heard that one before."

"But I really mean it this time. I've had it with him."

That evening at dinnertime, Voytek's antics were all anyone could talk about.

"He's better than an acrobat," Stanislav said proudly.

"We could always sell him to a circus," Pavel suggested.

"And we'll throw in that monkey for free," Janusz added.

"Where is Voytek, by the way?" Lolek asked.

"No idea. Peter said he was going to chain him up, didn't you, Peter?" Stanislav said. Peter closed his eyes and sighed. He told the others that he would definitely put Voytek on the chain that night. Or, if not, then tomorrow for certain.

"Promise?" said Stanislav.

"Promise," said Peter.

14

Voytek was enjoying a beer with the other soldiers. Peter tried to pull the bottle from his paws, but he had no chance. Voytek held onto his bottle and lifted it high in the air so that Peter couldn't reach it.

The sky was full of stars and the moon hung above the mountaintops, like a boat at anchor. Soldiers sang and joked in the camp. The air was full of new sounds: crickets, midges, an owl, and the noise of soldiers laughing, which no one had heard for a long time.

The men from the transport company of the 2nd Polish Corps drank to victory. Together with their allies, they had chased the enemy from the mountains of southern Italy. The road to Rome was finally open.

The Germans had retreated a long way, back toward their own country. Maybe it wasn't quite far enough yet, but at least now the allies were making progress.

"We can breathe freely, at least for a while," Pavel said.

"Yeah," Stanislav agreed. "If a bomb didn't get us, the stink of sauerkraut would soon have finished us all off."

"Don't get too excited. There's still a long way to go," said Lolek.

"Hey, Lollie, don't go spoiling it for us. We can celebrate for one evening, can't we?" Stanislav said.

"If you can call this a celebration," Lolek muttered.

But no one heard what Lolek had said, because all of the soldiers were looking up at the sergeant, who had suddenly emerged from the darkness. Sergeant Kowalski had come to tell them that the whole company had to line up at eight o'clock the next morning. The colonel was coming to inspect the troops and Kowalski wanted his men to have everything in tiptop shape. Shoes, buttons, weapons — everything had to shine.

"Men!" he finally shouted. "I don't want to see any sleepy or unshaven faces. And make sure that bear behaves himself." He nodded at Peter as he gave that last order.

"At your command, sergeant," said Lolek.

"You are such a bootlicker," Stanislav said to Lolek when the sergeant had gone.

Peter told them to stop squabbling, but Stanislav said Lolek was spoiling everyone's fun.

"First he doesn't want us to celebrate, and then he's trying to get into Kowalski's good graces. It makes me sick. Anyone would think he was a Kraut."

Lolek stood up slowly and walked over to Stanislav with his fists clenched. No one had seen him with that look on his face before.

"What did you just say?" Lolek said. It was almost a whisper, but everyone heard, because suddenly the whole place was deathly quiet. Only the crickets paid no attention and just carried on, chirping away.

A few days earlier, when the fighting had been at its worst, Lolek had gone out by himself in the jeep to pick up two soldiers from another camp. A straightforward job. A piece of cake, he thought. When Lolek arrived at the pick-up point, the two soldiers were already waiting for him. They waved as he came around the corner.

But suddenly there was a deafening bang. The air, the

ground, everything shook. Flames shot up into the sky and then it started raining mud, stones, grit, and branches. Lolek curled up in his seat with his arms around his head. The jeep's windshield turned black. The grit had blasted everything. Lolek could even feel it crunching between his teeth.

He got out of the jeep and ran into the army camp for help. But no help was needed, because there was nothing left of the two soldiers who had been standing there just a second before, waving at him. A shell had landed right at their feet.

That afternoon, Lolek drove back to his own camp. He reported to the commanding officer, but he didn't tell anyone else what had happened. What could he say to them? It was all part and parcel of war, wasn't it? No one was going to cry over one soldier more or less. What mattered was survival. Once you were dead, you didn't count. You'd already lost.

But now he was standing there in front of Stanislav, with his fists clenched, and Stanislav could see that he was serious.

"Sorry," he said, "I didn't . . ." But he got no further than that.

"Do you know," Lolek yelled, "how many people have already been blown up for nothing?"

"Sorry, Lolek," Stanislav tried again.

"Do you know how many lives this war has already cost?"

"Calm down. I was just having a laugh."

"Do you know what it feels like to see two boys standing there and then getting blown to pieces the next second, with bits of them hanging from the trees?"

"What on earth are you talking about?"

"I'm talking about this celebration, this party, that you're trying to have this evening. The celebration that isn't a celebration. I'm talking about the boys I was supposed to pick up a couple of days ago, who'd be sitting here with us now if I'd been just five minutes earlier."

The other soldiers all gaped at Lolek. They asked him which boys he was talking about, but Lolek looked down at his feet and didn't say anything. His fists were still clenched.

No one moved, but then Lolek felt something shove against his back. It was the bear, rubbing his huge head between Lolek's shoulder blades.

Voytek stood up on his back legs and positioned himself between Lolek and Stanislav, like a father trying to separate his sons.

"Lol," Stanislav said gently. "Hey, Lol, why are you only telling us this now?" Voytek stayed where he was, looking at Lolek, then at Stanislav, and back again.

"They were younger than me," Lolek said. "It's so unfair."

"War is unfair," Stanislav answered.

"Whenever I close my eyes, I can see those two soldiers waving at me," Lolek continued.

Peter walked over to him. So did Janusz and Pavel. They patted Lolek on the back.

"And when I open my eyes, they're gone. They were supposed to be waiting for me, but a shell came along instead." Lolek's expression had returned to normal and his knuckles were no longer white.

Everyone stood in silence for a moment. Then Peter said, "I saw a boot a while ago and it still had a chunk of someone's

leg in it." Some of the soldiers swore when they heard that.

"And do you know what I saw the other day?" Pavel said. "A dead soldier with a cigarette in his mouth. And it was still lit. He was lying on his side, like he was having a nap, but there was a fresh bullet in his head."

"Jeez," Stanislav sighed. "You know what, Lolek? You could see it this way: if you'd been five minutes earlier, the soldiers might be alive now — but if you'd been just one minute earlier, bits of you would be hanging in the trees, just like those other two soldiers, and they'd have been try-ing to work out which bits belonged to which soldier."

Lolek nodded.

"Not that there'd be any point," Stanislav said. "You can't save a dead man."

Lolek nodded again. "It's just not easy, that's all," he said finally.

"Those are true words. War's not easy." Stanislav stubbed out his cigarette with his boot, gave Lolek's shoulder a squeeze and went to his tent.

The others did the same: they finished smoking their cigarettes, patted Lolek on the back and headed for their beds. It was going to be an early start tomorrow, because they had to get everything ready for the colonel's inspection.

When Lolek was curled up in his bed, he heard a shuffling outside his tent. He went to see what it was and found Voytek pushing his nose under the tent flap and wriggling his way into the tent. That night, Voytek didn't sleep with Peter for once, but snuggled up next to Lolek instead.

15

The men lined up in neat rows the next morning. When the colonel arrived, all of the soldiers sprang to attention. Not only the privates, but the sergeants, the lieutenants, and the commanding officer too — everyone saluted when the high-ranking soldier with his chest covered with medals stepped out of his jeep.

The only one scratching away at his belly was Private Voytek.

"Stop that!" Peter hissed at him and he tugged the beautiful red rope that he'd tied around Voytek's neck for the special occasion.

But Voytek had no idea why he shouldn't have a nice scratch. What was so bad about scratching?

The colonel walked around, inspecting the troops. He nodded here and there, gave a crisp salute and walked along the rows of soldiers, with perfect military posture.

When he saw Voytek, he stopped.

"Ah, it's our ammunition carrier," he said. The serious expression on his face melted away. He walked up to Voytek, who instantly stopped his shameless scratching, much to Peter's relief. The colonel said he'd heard a great deal about this very special bear and that he was very pleased to finally meet him in person.

The company's C.O., Captain Brozek, who was accompanying the colonel, proudly explained that Voytek was an official member of the 2nd Polish Corps.

The colonel laughed and nodded and said, very loudly, so that all the soldiers could hear him, "I will personally ensure that this soldier is never forgotten." Then he walked on and continued his inspection.

"What does he mean?" whispered Stanislav.

"No idea," Peter replied.

The commanding officer glared at the two soldiers and they stopped talking. That morning, the C.O. had spoken very sternly to his men. "No matter what happens," he said, "you will remain standing at attention. Even if the wind is force twelve and the tents are flying through the air, even if hailstones the size of bullets are falling from the sky, you will not move a muscle. And you will not make a sound. Understood?"

"Understood, captain!" the soldiers had chorused.

In perfect silence, the soldiers stood at ease while the colonel went off to inspect the tents, the trucks, the cookhouse, and the weapons. It all took so long that Voytek yawned and sat down.

Peter and Stanislav stared straight ahead, like all the others, until a ripple suddenly ran through the rows. All the soldiers turned around.

First the commanding officer came running up, followed by the colonel. They suddenly realized that he was completely bald! But before they could start to wonder what had happened to his beret, Stalin came galloping by. On his back sat Kaska the monkey. One of her paws held onto Stalin's collar and the other was holding the colonel's beret on her head.

The story spread like wildfire: "That monkey dropped down from a tree and stole the colonel's beret!" The men

started laughing quietly and before long no one was standing neatly in position. They were all craning their necks so they wouldn't have to miss any of the fun.

"Atteeeeen-tion!" the commanding officer yelled, furiously. He ordered one of the soldiers to chase after Kaska. When the soldier came back a little later, without Kaska, but with the beret, the C.O. was still fuming.

The soldiers listened as he apologized to the colonel, over and over again. His face was dripping with sweat.

The colonel waved aside the C.O.'s apologies and said, "You should start a circus."

"Do what?" the C.O. said, his face bright red.

"Start a circus," the colonel repeated.

There was laughter in the ranks.

The C.O. hissed at his men. "Remember what I told you! Silence! No matter what!"

The soldiers pulled themselves together and stared straight ahead.

"A circus? Why would you say that?" the C.O. asked. He sounded almost offended.

"Well, it seems obvious to me," the colonel replied. He was looking directly at Stanislav as he spoke.

Stanislav stood up even straighter and said, "Yes, captain, the colonel means that you wouldn't put yourself to shame as a circus director with a show starring a bear that carries artillery shells and a monkey in a beret galloping around in circles on a dog."

For a moment, there was absolute silence. Lolek was so nervous that he almost fainted and Peter forgot to breathe. Stanislav was so shocked by his own behavior that he suddenly started shaking like a leaf.

"Exactly," the colonel bellowed at the C.O. "That's precisely what I meant. When the war's over, you can take these animals of yours on the road. You already have a tent. All you need to do is decorate it, add a bit of sand and sawdust — and you're all set!"

Now all the soldiers started to laugh. The colonel saluted one last time, gave Stanislav an almost imperceptible wink, climbed back into his jeep and left.

"Lubanski!" the commanding officer yelled as soon as the colonel was out of sight. "Come here!"

Stanislav walked up to the front and stood before his C.O.

"No matter what happens, I said. Even if the tents are flying around your ears, even if we're flattened by a deadly hailstorm, you stay where you are and you don't make a sound."

"Yes, captain," Stanislav said.

"Even if a monkey gallops past on a dog, not a sound."

"Yes, captain," Stanislav repeated.

"And even if the monkey's wearing the colonel's beret on her head, not a sound."

"Yes, captain."

"And when the colonel's talking to me, most certainly not a single sound!"

"Got it, sir," Stanislav said.

"Have you got that?" the C.O. said.

"That's what I just said, captain."

"If you think you're so clever, Lubanski, you can find a solution for our monkey problem. Today. I don't care what it is. Just come up with something. As far as I'm concerned, you can use your gun on it, but I'll tell you one thing: the next time that monkey bothers me, I'm holding you responsible. Is that clear?"

"Yes, sir." Stanislav turned on his heels and went back to stand between Voytek and Lolek.

"Tomorrow we're leaving for Rome," the C.O. shouted at the men. "Make sure you're ready in good time. Your sergeant will give you further orders. Dismissed!" He was back to being his bossy old self and handing out one order after another. His booming voice could be heard in every corner of the camp.

"Lol, what are we going to do about that monkey?" Stanislav said as they were walking back to their tent. "Didn't you have an idea once?"

"Yeah, Kaska needs a man," Lolek said.

"Oh yes, I remember now. That was your bright idea!" Stanislav threw his arms in the air and looked around. "Would you like to tell me where we're going to find a male monkey among these ruins?"

"There's a zoo in Rome," Lolek replied.

"Not likely. No way Brozek's going to go for that," said Stanislav.

"I'll go with you," Lolek said.

"Well? Well?" Peter, Pavel, and Janusz all asked at the same time when they saw Lolek and Stanislav returning from their visit to the C.O.

"It's all sorted out!" Stanislav said with a laugh. "And if I didn't have Lollie, I'd still be stuck with a very big problem." He pointed at his gun and said, "Shooting a sauerkraut-cruncher sounds just about manageable, but a monkey? Who could shoot a monkey?" He shook his head, grabbed Lolek, and gave him a big kiss on his cheek.

The next morning, the soldiers of the transport company of the 2nd Polish Corps headed out of the mountains of Monte Cassino. They drove around craters and past walls of barbed wire. They saw burned-out tanks, scraps of tent canvas, helmets, empty cartridges, water bottles, and the occasional dead horse. Wherever they looked, there was rubble, rubble, and more rubble.

So how was it possible for poppies to be blooming everywhere? Some fields seemed to be entirely red.

"From our blood," Pavel said after a while. The others nodded and gazed at the thousands of flowers waving in the breeze.

"One for every soldier," Lolek said. Then everyone in the truck fell silent, as it began to sink in just how hard the battle must have been for the soldiers at the front.

When Rome came into sight, the soldiers started talking again. Finally, they were in a place that hadn't been looted and shot to pieces. Thank God the Eternal City was still standing.

"That's good news for us, eh?" Lolek said.

"What do you mean?" Stanislav asked.

Lolek pointed at the undamaged buildings and said, "If the city's still standing, then the zoo's probably still intact."

The soldiers took up their quarters in their new camp just outside the city. Toward the end of the afternoon, the commanding officer gave Stanislav and Lolek official leave so they could take a drive to the zoo. They fetched Kaska, climbed into a jeep, and headed for the center of Rome.

The zoo director gave Lolek and Stanislav a warm reception. "Welcome to our zoo," he said. "How very nice it is to have some visitors. And with such an unusual request, too."

Lolek and Stanislav were puzzled, but the director explained that he'd received a telephone call from the army camp. "Captain Brozek told me that two of his men were on their way here with a female monkey," he said.

The two soldiers looked at the director in surprise.

"Our commanding officer called you about this himself?" Stanislav asked.

"He most certainly did," the director replied. "And as you helped to liberate Rome, I'd be very happy to do you a favor in return." The director looked at Kaska, who was sitting sweetly on Lolek's lap. "And I think I'll be able to help, because we have a male of her species in our collection." He smiled at the men and Kaska as he rang a bell on his desk. Before long, one of the zookeepers came to his office.

"This young lady's coming to stay with us for a week," the director told him. "She's to be treated with respect and introduced to a male companion of her species as soon as possible."

The zookeeper nodded at the director and walked over to pick Kaska up. As soon as he touched her, though, she started screaming and held on tight to Lolek's uniform. Her eyes were full of panic. It was a real effort for the keeper to tear Kaska away from Lolek's lap. She bit him and she hit him. Even the director had never seen such an angry monkey before.

"What a vicious little lady," he said, but Lolek and Stanislav barely heard. They were watching with concern as the keeper carried Kaska away. When Kaska realized the soldiers weren't coming with her, she stopped screaming and anxiously clung to the keeper.

"Ow," they heard the keeper yelling as he headed down the corridor. "Ow, you mean little monkey, let go of my hair!"

Lolek gave a deep sigh when they were back outside.

"Come on," said Stanislav, "let's go and have an ice cream cone. I think we've earned it."

It was June 1944 and the evening sun gently descended on the red rooftops of the city. They both bought a lemon ice cream cone and wandered along the narrow streets of old Rome. Lolek and Stanislav looked like a couple of tourists as they gazed at the city's statues and fountains. And of course they didn't look only at the statues and fountains, but also at the girls with their bare legs and their long, loose hair.

"Do you know what we should do?" Stanislav said. "Let's drive back to the camp, report to Brozek, and then pick up the others and come back to Rome."

"What a great idea," said Lolek. And he looked happy for the first time in ages.

16

As they were waiting for new orders, the whole company had been given furlough. The men didn't have to report to the army camp in Rome for a whole week. They were allowed to do whatever they wanted, as long as they behaved themselves.

Peter, Stanislav, Pavel, Janusz, Lolek, and Voytek headed off on a trip in an army truck. Voytek hung his head out of the window, as always, and when they came close to a village and he smelled an orchard full of peach trees, his nostrils started to quiver with pleasure.

"Do you want to ask them if we can stay here?" Stanislav said.

Peter drove the truck up the sandy road and parked in front of the farmhouse. Stanislav jumped down from the cab and went over to knock on the door. He soon came back with a grin on his face and pointed at the orchard. The soldiers were allowed to pitch their tents there.

"But I didn't mention that we have a . . . um . . . rather overgrown pet with us," Stanislav said.

When they'd put the tents up and Voytek was safely on his chain, the whole family came to take a look. They'd brought some food to welcome the soldiers.

They were scared out of their wits when they saw Voytek, but after Peter had given him a tickle and Stanislav had made him do a headstand, everything was fine. The farmer's wife even told the soldiers they could eat as many

peaches as they wanted.

It was the height of summer and Voytek spent the whole day sunbathing and drowsing in the grass. When the soldiers weren't patching up their truck, they were usually lying beside Voytek, or visiting the village for a beer.

Voytek was like a new bear. Days and days of rain had left his coat hanging on him like a soaked rug most of the time, but now it began to gleam again, and he looked a little fatter every day.

They were guests on the farm, where all sorts of animals were wandering around, so Peter made absolutely certain that Voytek was chained up at all times.

"Look at the way he's staring at those chickens," he said to the others one morning. "I think he might have

discovered his hunting instinct." As soon as Voytek realized that Peter was keeping an eye on him, he started to act as though the chickens didn't exist, but when Peter looked the other way, he immediately starting spying on them again.

"There's no way we can let Voytek off that chain," Peter said to everyone, particularly Stanislav. "I would die of shame if he ran riot and turned the farm upside down."

But Stanislav said that the butterball had no chance of getting his paws on any of the animals. He was right about the chickens: they steered well clear of Voytek. But their chicks didn't recognize the largely immobile heap of fur as a threat. They scratched around in the grass, getting closer and closer to Voytek. And when one of the chicks went chasing around after a breadcrumb and came within a few feet of Voytek, he quickly stirred himself and pounced on the chick, narrowly missing it.

The cackling of the chickens and the rattling of Voytek's chain alerted the soldiers. Peter was under the truck, welding a hole in the muffler, when it happened. He banged his head as he pulled himself out from beneath the truck. Cursing and waving his fists, he ran over to Voytek. But Voytek just lay there as though nothing had happened.

When Peter saw that all of the chicks were still alive, he rubbed his head and cursed again.

"Do you know what? We're going to have to spy on

him," Stanislav said when they'd finished the lunch that Janusz had prepared for them. All of the soldiers hid behind the barn, where they had a good view of what Voytek got up to when he was on his own. They saw him lying down in the grass, like a good bear, but they also noticed that his eyes were very slightly open. He was carefully watching the chicks through a very small slit.

Slowly, they came pecking along toward him. Voytek didn't move a muscle. He held his food bowl in his paws and waited until the chicks were very close.

Then, in a burst of movement, Voytek stood up and slammed his bowl down over the chicks.

"Nooo!" Peter cried.

"You have to admit it — that is a very clever bear," Stanislav said with a laugh.

They watched the contented expression on Voytek's face as he looked down at his upturned bowl. A cheeping sound came from beneath it and the mother hen soon joined in with her cackling.

Peter was about to run over to Voytek, but Stanislav stopped him. "Let's just wait and see what he does," he whispered.

"We're guests here. Remember?" Peter hissed.

"Just stay calm," said Stanislav. "There's no way Voytek's going to eat those little chicks."

"Yes, but all he needs to do is give them a pat with one of those big paws of his and he'll crush them."

Before anyone could reply, the soldiers saw that Voytek was carefully picking up the bowl and slowly trying to push his nose under the edge. That nose was quite a bit bigger than the chicks, and when Voytek had squeezed it under the bowl, there was enough room for the chicks to rush out and run back to their mother.

Voytek looked around in dismay. When the soldiers walked over to him, laughing, he dropped his bowl and looked in the other direction.

"You funny bear," said Peter.

"Idiot," said Stanislav with a grin. And they jumped onto his back.

"What a big brave bear," Peter said.

"Chasing after tiny little chicks!" Stanislav said.

But Voytek didn't react. He looked up at the sky and acted as though no one was sitting on his back.

Voytek behaved himself so well the rest of the week that they gave him a little more freedom on the last day of the break. The soldiers could see he'd given up the hope of a tasty meal, so they made the chain a bit longer.

They had to report to the army camp in Rome the next day and they decided to spend their last free evening at the movies. Just as they were climbing into the truck, the farmer's son came running up.

"The bear! The bear!" he shouted in Italian. But even if he'd been shouting in Chinese, the soldiers would have known that something was very wrong and that they needed to make a swift about-face.

Peter flew straight to Voytek, who was peacefully sleeping in the grass. The boy was still yelling at them, but they couldn't understand what he was saying. He kept pointing at Voytek, though, so they knew it must be something to do with him.

Voytek pretended not to hear anything, even when Peter called his name.

"Strange," he said.

"Very mysterious," agreed Stanislav, who had joined him. "He doesn't usually lie on his stomach."

"You don't think he's sick, do you?" Lolek asked.

"If he was sick, he'd be making a real fuss," Peter said thoughtfully. "No, that bear's definitely up to no good." Peter walked over to Voytek and gave him a prod. Nothing happened. Voytek just lay there, perfectly still, and kept his eyes shut.

"Be quiet for a moment," Peter said. The soldiers heard a strange noise coming from Voytek's stomach. It wasn't a rumble, or a cheep.

"A death rattle," Stanislav exclaimed.

Peter grabbed Voytek's chain, tugged it, and shouted at the top of his voice: "Voytek, stand up! Right now!" Voytek jumped to his feet. And a goose waddled out from beneath his stomach. It looked very ruffled and little white feathers were floating through the air.

The boy jumped up and down happily when he saw that the goose was safe and unharmed.

"We're too late for the movie now," Stanislav said.

"So let's go for a beer in the village square instead," Peter replied. Before they left, they made the chain a lot shorter, so short that Voytek could barely move. Secretly, though, they were a little bit proud of their cunning bear.

"What do you think he was planning to do to that goose?" Stanislav wondered aloud.

"No idea," said Peter, "but it was a smart move."

"To Voytek," they said, clinking their glasses and taking a swig of beer.

"And to Kaska," Lolek added, taking another swig. "I wonder how she's getting along."

The other soldiers all joined in with his toast. "To Kaska!"

17

The next morning, the five soldiers reluctantly packed up their things. The beer had given them thick heads and all they really wanted was to sleep for a few more hours. They didn't wake the sixth soldier until it was actually time to go.

"Back to work," Peter said as Voytek climbed into the truck.

Stanislav pretended to be a machine gun and jabbed at Voytek's fur with his finger. "Ratatatata!" Voytek ignored the soldiers and concentrated on trying to open up the box in the cab where the soldiers always kept a few goodies.

"Here you go," said Peter, giving Voytek a piece of bread.

"And how about a nice cup of joe?" said Stanislav, passing Voytek the flask of coffee.

"Idiot!" Peter snapped. "That's way too hot."

"What? And those cigarettes of his aren't?" Stanislav replied. He'd barely finished the sentence before Voytek had glugged down the entire flask of coffee.

When they got back to the army camp at the end of the afternoon, the guard put his head in through the truck window. "Private Lubanski?" he said to Stanislav.

"Yes, what is it?" Stanislav asked.

"The C.O. wants you to report to his office."

A short while later, Stanislav came back to his friends, with something in his arms.

"Kaska!" Peter exclaimed. Stanislav told them that the

zoo director couldn't keep her there any longer, because she kept smashing things up and screeching her head off.

"Brozek says she's my responsibility now."

Stanislav sat down, put Kaska on the chair beside him and said, "There's only one thing for it."

"What do you mean?" Peter asked.

Stanislav made a gun out of his index finger and thumb and said, "Bang!"

"You wouldn't dare," said Pavel.

"Oh yeah?" Stanislav replied. "There's already a war on and with that monkey around, it'll be like two wars at the same time." He picked up his gun and aimed it at Kaska. She screeched and looked anxiously down the barrel and started bouncing up and down on the chair.

"Just give her to me," Lolek said. Without waiting for an answer, he picked Kaska up.

"What about Voytek?" said Peter. "What's it going to be like with the two of them?"

"We'll have to wait and see," Lolek said.

"Just as long as they keep out of my supplies," said Janusz.

"Does this mean you're taking responsibility for her from now on?" asked Stanislav.

Lolek nodded, stood up, raised two fingers in the air, and solemnly said, "I, Leonard Zebrowski, private in the 2nd Polish Corps, assigned to the transport company, do hereby swear to take complete responsibility for looking after Kaska, the little monkey no one wants, who has just escaped the firing squad by the skin of her teeth."

All that time, Kaska sat calmly on Lolek's left arm, tugging the buttons of his shirt and gently rubbing his nose.

"Do you know what you're getting yourself into?"

Stanislav said, but he looked so relieved that Lolek laughed and said, "Well, I think I could already do with a good strong coffee." Stanislav went straight to work and made coffee for everyone.

"Thanks, Lol," he said. "You do know I'd never really pull the trigger, don't you?" But before Lolek could reply, the unsuspecting Voytek came wandering over. He'd been having afternoon tea with the neighbors — you could tell by the crumbs on his face. When he saw Kaska, he stiffened, sat down on his haunches, and covered his eyes with his paws.

Kaska let go of Lolek's buttons and jumped out of his arms. She bounded over to Voytek, hopped up onto his back and gave his ears a few good hard tugs. Then she darted off like an arrow. It all happened in just a few seconds and before anyone could do anything, Kaska had disappeared.

Voytek just shook his head. Lolek looked at his empty arms as if he couldn't believe what had just happened.

He got up to look for Kaska, but he couldn't find her anywhere. Stanislav helped him to look and Janusz and Pavel joined in the search after dinner. Even Peter hoped that Kaska would turn up soon. Once you've welcomed your enemy into your home, it's a good idea to make sure you know where that enemy is at all times.

Lolek didn't sleep a wink that night. He had sworn an oath and he intended to keep his promise. He had to find Kaska before they left the army camp the next morning.

An hour before sunrise, Lolek went out looking for Kaska again, but he still couldn't find her, no matter where he looked. By then, the other soldiers had all started taking down their tents.

"Come on, Lolek," they said to him, "we're leaving in half an hour." All Lolek could do was pack up his things and grab some breakfast.

When the soldiers met at the trucks half an hour later, Stanislav suddenly shouted, "Hey, would you take a look at that?"

An enormous dog came loping out of the early-morning mist. Regally, he galloped up to the soldiers. A small rider was perched on the dog's back, a rider with a grin that stretched from the north of Italy to the south. Like a seasoned cavalryman, Kaska dug her heels into Stalin's sides when she saw the soldiers.

"Here!" Lolek called. Stalin obediently trotted over to Lolek and stopped at his feet. Lolek picked up Kaska and climbed into the truck with Pavel and Janusz.

"We can go!" he cried. And off they went, in a convoy, jerking and shuddering along the roads, which had been shot to pieces. The men from the transport company were on their way to their next mission. And no matter how difficult that mission was, every mile took them closer to home.

18

Lolek was awakened in the middle of the night by something tapping his head. It was Kaska. She'd climbed onto his chest and was hitting his face with her little fists, as though she wanted to say: come on, wake up, open your eyes!

"Go to sleep, Kaska," Lolek said, but Kaska kept on beating her fists on his head and screeching at him.

Lolek picked up his flashlight and shone it around the tent. Then he aimed it at Kaska. She was rubbing her tummy and shaking her head.

"Come here, you," Lolek said. He grabbed Kaska and rocked her in his arms for a while. The rain rattled down on the tent. It soon started to thunder too.

"Ssshh," Lolek said. "Ssshh, Kaska, don't be scared." He snuggled back under the blankets and gave Kaska a hug. "Sssshhh," he kept saying, until she finally began to calm down. The two of them went back to sleep.

When the dawn light came creeping under the tent flap, Kaska started whimpering again. The thunderstorm was long gone by then and Lolek could tell from the light that the sky was clear. Kaska crawled to another corner of the tent and Lolek turned over.

He didn't know if he went back to sleep after that, but suddenly he sat upright. "You idiot," he whispered to himself. He got out of bed and searched all of the hiding places in the tent until he found Kaska.

She was huddled up on his uniform jacket, which she'd made into a nest. Lolek's jaw dropped. Kaska was holding a furry little bundle to her chest and when Lolek came closer she lifted it up for him to take a look. "A son," he whispered. "Kaska, you have a little son."

Lolek stroked Kaska's back and said, "Good, Kaska, good." He kept repeating the words, over and over again, as if they were the only words in the world. And Kaska looked at Lolek with an expression he'd never seen before. It was almost as if the monkey had new eyes, a new nose, and a new mouth. Everything about her shone and gleamed.

"Your little boy has the same wrinkled face as my uncle Jakobus," Lolek whispered. He smiled and knew that he'd found the perfect name for Kaska's baby. He'd call him Kubus.

"Kubus is the pet name for Jakobus," Lolek explained. "Just like Kaska's short for Katarina. Bet you didn't know that, eh?" And Lolek just kept on chatting away to Kaska. He couldn't take his eyes off the monkeys.

It may be war outside, he thought, but here, in my tent, we finally have a little bit of peace.

Lolek felt so far away from reality that it was like waking up from a dream when he heard someone shouting outside his tent. Stanislav was calling him.

"Hey, Lollie! Wake up! It's almost time to go back to bed again. What are you up to in there?"

"Sssh," Lolek said. He took another quick look at Kaska and Kubus to make sure he hadn't dreamed it and then put his head through the tent flaps to tell the others to keep the noise down.

Then he allowed them into the tent, one by one, to admire Kubus. Stanislav went out and told the news to everyone he met, even soldiers he didn't know. "Remember that pesky little monkey? She's had a baby, a tiny little worm of a thing!" And he held his thumb and forefinger a very short distance apart to show them just how small the baby was.

"You're so proud that anyone would think you'd become a father yourself," Peter said. Stanislav just shrugged and said someone had to pass on the good news. Lolek didn't have the time to tell everyone — he had to guard the tent, because otherwise it would have been stormed by the entire division of the 2nd Polish Corps, all coming to visit the baby monkey.

Even the commanding officer came to take a look.

"Congratulations, Zebrowski," he said, "taking her to

the zoo was a brilliant plan. Let's just hope the little one's not as much of a pain in the neck as his mother!"

The next day, Kaska left the tent. Everyone had another chance to look at Kubus. And Kaska ran up and showed Kubus to anyone who didn't come to look. She even made Stalin take a sniff of Kubus. It was the first time the soldiers had seen that huge horse of a dog wag his tail.

When Kaska spotted Voytek and the dalmatian, she made a beeline for them, but Voytek dashed into Peter's tent with the dalmatian close on his heels. It was a month before Voytek realized he didn't need to run away from Kaska anymore, and another month before he finally dared to take his paws off his eyes and take a look at what Kaska kept trying to show him.

He growled very gently when Kaska held Kubus up to him. But Voytek wasn't looking at Kubus. He took a good, long look at Kaska. It was probably the first time he'd ever really looked at her.

Then, finally, he looked at Kubus. He almost had to cross his eyes to see the little monkey, because Kaska had pushed her son right up against Voytek's nose — a nose that was almost bigger than the little monkey himself. And suddenly Voytek felt a tiny little hand reach out and give his nose a good, hard pinch.

He sat up on his haunches and took another look from a safe distance. He didn't notice that the soldiers had already loaded up their trucks and were about to leave the camp. But then someone blew a horn and he scooted off.

"Where did you get to?" Peter said. "We thought you'd decided to take the day off."

Voytek stopped at the truck door and peered back over

his shoulder, with a strange look on his face, as though he'd only just realized what he'd seen.

"Hurry up, bear," Peter said. But Voytek didn't move an inch. He kept staring over his shoulder.

"What is it now?" shouted Stanislav.

Kaska came ambling along through the tents. Voytek didn't put his paws over his eyes, but turned around and watched Kaska until she disappeared from sight. Peter and Stanislav realized that the feud was finally over.

"Now we've just got the Germans to sort out," Stanislav said with a sigh, "and we then can all go home."

19

It was still dark when Voytek crept out of Peter's tent. He took one look around and darted back inside, startling Peter awake in the process, because he wasn't exactly quiet.

"Voy, what are you doing?" Peter yelled. It was so dark in the tent that he couldn't see a thing, but he felt Voytek sliding back under the covers.

The bear was wet and freezing cold. Peter gave him a shove and told him to get out of bed. He lay down and Voytek waddled back out of the tent. This time he didn't come back.

Peter tried to get back to sleep, but he couldn't, because Voytek was kicking up such an unholy racket right outside his tent. He got dressed and went to see what all the noise was about. He understood as soon as he opened the tent flap. The earth was white and almost glowing.

"Snow," he whispered. Voytek was nowhere to be seen, but Peter could tell from the tracks in the snow just how wildly he'd been leaping about.

It was six o'clock by then and time to get up. One by one, sleepy and surprised faces looked out at the snow. Fall was at an end and the night had brought winter with it.

The C.O. gave the men from the transport company their new orders over breakfast in the mess tent. He told them they had to put chains on their tires before they set off or they'd go sliding off the road, like a sled. They didn't have any chains, so they'd have to borrow some from the

British soldiers, which meant that the company couldn't start work yet.

After breakfast, the soldiers went looking for Voytek. They wanted to see what their bear was up to in the snow. It wasn't hard to find him. He was a big brown beast in a perfectly white world.

They could already see Voytek in the distance, running around in the snow. He was chasing the dalmatian and when he caught him, the two of them rolled around together, with the snow dusting up around them. The dalmatian was barking so much that clouds of steam had formed around his head. His white fur vanished against the backdrop of snow and sometimes all you could see was a collection of black dots dancing happily around.

"Dottiiieee!" Stanislav called, when he saw the dalmatian. "Where are you? Where are you?" And the dalmatian raced over to him, as though he was saying, "Here I am! Here I am!" Stanislav grabbed the dog and ruffled his head and said, "I can't see you, just a patch of dots bouncing around. Where have you gone, Dottie?"

Voytek came dashing over too. He had to brake so hard that he slipped on the snow and took Stanislav sliding along with him. The dalmatian jumped on top of them, and there was just a whirling mass of fur, dots, and khaki clothes spinning through the snow.

Pavel, Janusz, Lolek, and Peter came to Stanislav's rescue. They pulled him to his feet and started piling armfuls of snow over Voytek and the dalmatian. Before long, a snowball fight between humans and animals started, with the humans quickly gaining the upper hand — until something hit Stanislav right between the eyes.

Kaska had arrived. She was sitting up high on the roof

of a truck and scraping together handfuls of snow, which she then rolled into rock-hard snowballs. Every snowball she threw hit its target. Of course it did, because Kaska was a perfect shot.

"Hey, you!" Stanislav shouted at her. "Do I look like a German?" The words were barely out of his mouth when another direct hit struck home, right between the eyes.

Kubus was up there too, sitting beside Kaska. He was trying to make snowballs like his mother. But when he went to throw one, he slipped off the truck and landed on the ground below, with his snowball on top of him.

Voytek darted after him and sniffed at the little monkey, which was wriggling around in the snow. Kubus screeched and flailed about, which only made him sink deeper into the chilly whiteness.

Voytek scooped up a great big pile in his big paws: Kubus, plus a whole load of snow. He held his paws up to his nose and started licking away.

Kaska bounced down from the truck and stood at Voytek's feet, jumping up and down and screeching.

The snowball fight had stopped and everyone watched this strange scene. Even the dalmatian was just lying down in the snow, panting away. It looked as though someone had been throwing black confetti around.

Lolek wondered out loud if the snow might be a bit cold for a baby monkey.

"Of course not," the others said. "He's covered in fur."

"But," Lolek said, "have you ever seen a monkey in the snow before?"

"Yes," Stanislav said. "What's more, I've seen two monkeys in the snow. Right now, in fact."

The others laughed and told Lolek not to worry so much. And if it was really a problem, couldn't he just find them some clothes?

Kaska had retrieved Kubus by then and she ran over to Stalin, who had also come over to take a look. She climbed onto his back and the three of them headed off somewhere. Stalin trotted this time, because there hadn't been any galloping since Kubus arrived.

"She's like a little monkey Mary on her donkey," Stanislav said, pointing at Kaska. "All that's missing is Joseph. Would you like to volunteer, Mr. Bear?" Stanislav gave Voytek a nudge, but Voytek didn't understand and shoved him back. Stanislav stumbled and fell over, and the fight started all over again.

The next few days, the soldiers had all the time they wanted for snowball fights, because the winter had put a stop to the war. The snow made it impossible to drive down the roads, and that was probably a good thing. They were getting low on supplies and they didn't have enough soldiers either. The British, Americans, and Poles needed more reinforcements before they could finally finish off the Germans.

One morning in early spring, a pale and worried-looking Lolek appeared in the mess tent. The birds were singing again and the snow had given way to mud. The troops had reinforcements and the men from the transport company had started driving back up and down to the port to restock the dwindling supplies.

"There's something wrong with Kubus," Lolek said. He sat down and poured himself some coffee.

"What's the problem?" the others said.

Lolek told them that the little monkey had been a bit quiet for a few days, but this morning he was just lying there and barely moving.

"Where is he now?" Peter asked.

Lolek told them that Kaska had taken him out with her, but he thought they really needed to find a vet.

After breakfast, the soldiers went out with Lolek. Sergeant Kowalski's orders could wait.

They found Kaska sitting on Stalin's back. He was trudging around and around through the puddles, not going anywhere.

"Stalin!" Peter called, and the big beast obediently walked over to him. There was something mournful about his steps. Kaska had her arms wrapped tightly around Kubus and just stared at him.

When Stalin stopped in front of the soldiers, they could see that Kubus's eyes were shut and one of his arms was dangling limply. Kaska was desperately tweaking his face. But it was no good. Kubus was dead.

"Come on, Kaska," Lolek said quietly. His voice trembled. When he leaned forward to pick her up, Kaska jumped down from Stalin's back and ran away. She hugged Kubus to her chest and didn't look back.

The men went to work. Only Lolek stayed behind to look for Kaska. The hours passed and he'd already turned the whole camp upside down three times before he finally found her.

She was in Lolek's tent, hidden beneath a pile of clothes. Lolek kept on talking to her as he carefully removed the pieces of clothing from on top of her, one by one. Kaska was still holding onto Kubus, as though she knew she'd lose him forever if she let him go.

"He's already gone," Lolek kept telling her. "Give him to me, Kaska. Come on, Kaska, just let him go." Slowly, he reached out his hand. Kaska looked at him for the first time in a while. The gleam in her eyes had gone. Lolek had never felt so wretched during the entire war as he did at that moment.

He picked up Kaska, who was still holding Kubus, and rocked her in his arms. He was still sitting there like that when Stanislav and Peter came to get him for dinner.

Stanislav pulled Lolek to his feet and Peter took Kubus from Kaska's arms. No one said a word, because there was nothing to say.

From that day, Kaska refused to eat. She dragged herself around the camp and Voytek followed her everywhere. One time Peter even saw Voytek gently licking Kaska. And Kaska let him — not because she was enjoying it, but because she didn't notice.

Lolek called in the vet. They tried to cheer her up with games and tasty food, but they couldn't get through to her, no matter what they did. It was as if Kaska's soul had gone with Kubus and only her body was left behind.

Lolek wrapped her up in his jacket every night before bed and, one morning, when he went to wake her up, he found her still lying in the same position she'd been in the night before.

The soldiers buried Kaska beside Kubus in a place in the woods that the war seemed not to have reached, because the birds were still singing and the first spring flowers were coming up.

When Voytek realized what had happened, he stopped eating too. He rocked his big body to and fro and didn't even want to go in the truck anymore.

"Not you too?" Peter said on the fourth morning when Voytek refused to work.

"If a bomb gets you, that's okay," Stanislav said, "but a good soldier doesn't die of sadness." He prodded Voytek's stomach. Voytek just growled.

"Hey, old soldier! Do you hear what I'm saying? If everyone decides they've had enough of living, we might as well just pack up and go home."

Stanislav tried to pull Voytek up. "Come and help me!" he called to the others. The five of them dragged Voytek to the truck and pushed him inside.

"What now?" Peter said.

"To the beach," Stanislav replied. And the soldiers set off before they'd even had breakfast.

A strong wind blew on the coast. White-crested waves came crashing onto the sand.

"Come on, you! Out!" Stanislav said to Voytek. The bear reluctantly climbed down from the truck. The soldiers dragged him to the water and started splashing him, from head to toe. First he sat down in the surf, growling to himself, but when Stanislav took off his uniform and jumped onto him, he shook him off and dived after him into the waves.

When the soldiers saw that, they all got undressed and ran into the waves in their underwear. It was really still far too cold to swim, but this was all part of Operation Voytek. After that first dive, Voytek seemed to shake off his sadness and he splashed around in the water, plunging in again and again, as though he was in his element.

Some people came over to watch and they applauded from the beach. Perhaps the men and their furry friend were from a circus, but what was a circus doing in a war zone? When the men put on soldiers' uniforms and drove off in an army truck, it all made even less sense. But the soldiers didn't notice the confusion, because they were too busy shivering with cold.

"Coffee," Peter said, with blue lips. "That's what I want. How about you?" he asked Voytek.

"Hmmm, a nice ice-cold beer for me," Stanislav growled in a deep voice, speaking for his friend Voytek.

20

"Voytek, you crazy animal, where are you?!" Stanislav ran through the camp, stopping every few steps to call Voytek's name. But if Stanislav had thought about it, he would have known exactly where Voytek was and there would have been no need for him to run around like a headless chicken.

Voytek was in the cookhouse, together with the dalmatian and Stalin, who had become part of their little gang since Kaska had gone.

"Hey, Voytek, hi," Stanislav said when he'd finally found him. But Voytek didn't look up, because he was busy concentrating on the cook. If you didn't keep your wits about you, you might miss out on the goodies. Even worse: someone else might get them.

Stanislav stood right in front of him and started waving his arms around to get his attention. Voytek just growled.

"Please take them away," the cook shouted above the noise of the kitchen, "all three of them. They've been in here begging for food all morning."

"Well, give them something, then," Stanislav shouted back, and he started waving his arms at Voytek again. Voytek had no idea why Stanislav was waving and pointing at his beret.

"Look, Voytek, look!" Stanislav took his beret off his head and almost thrust it in Voytek's face. But Voytek just stared over the top of the beret at the cook and at the huge bowl of chopped meat and the pile of cheese sitting there on the counter, with no one keeping an eye on it.

Peter, Janusz, Pavel, and Lolek came running over too. "Voytek!" they shouted. "Voytek!" Voytek knew when he was beaten. And the soldiers had the attention of the dalmatian and Stalin now too. The dalmatian started barking and Stalin lay down and tilted his head, looking at the dancing soldiers with a serious expression on his doggy face.

"Champagne!" Peter called to the cook.

"Why? Have we finally sent the Germans packing?" he asked, slicing the onions with his flashing knife.

"Take a look!" Stanislav called, and when the cook saw what Stanislav was showing him, he dropped the knife, wiped his hands on his apron and ran out of the kitchen.

When he came back, he was carrying a bottle.

"I was actually saving this to celebrate victory," the cook said.

The bottle opened with a loud pop. None of the animals jumped, because they'd all heard much louder explosions before.

"But if this doesn't call for a celebration, I don't know what does," the cook continued. "And I don't know about you, but I can't bear to wait! Get it? Bear to wait!" The cook laughed at his own joke and asked Stanislav if he could take a closer look. He whistled in admiration as he studied Stanislav's beret.

On the beret was the new emblem of the transport company of the 2nd Polish Corps: a bear with an artillery shell in its paws.

The emblem was not only to be placed on all of the soldiers' berets and uniforms, but also painted on every single truck. The colonel who had come to inspect the troops

almost a year ago had kept his word. "I will personally ensure that this soldier is never forgotten," he had said.

The cook took the first swig of champagne, straight from the bottle. Then he passed it to Peter, and Peter passed it to Stanislav, who, without thinking, handed it to Voytek, and Voytek downed the rest of that very expensive luxury without leaving even a drop for the others.

"Thanks, Cookie," Stanislav said. He walked over to the counter, picked up a handful of hamburger meat and gave it to the dogs.

"You'll be getting spaghetti without sauce for dinner," the cook laughed.

"And now back to work," Peter said.

They climbed into their trucks to drive to the port. Ships arrived every day with ammunition and artillery parts. The final offensive was about to begin. The army needed bullets, mortars, grenades, and shells. And Voytek helped to carry everything and, of course, he still scared the living daylights out of people wherever they went.

The final offensive took four weeks in total. The Germans, who were hiding in the mountains, were bombarded on all sides, with machine gun fire and hundreds and hundreds of bombs dropping from planes. They fell from the sky like huge drops of rain and smashed the earth to pieces.

The rumbling and booming went on day and night. The fighting shifted closer and closer to Germany and the men from the transport company had to travel longer distances to reach their fellow soldiers on the front line.

They drove past crumbling churches and flattened forests, through barbed-wire barriers and along roads that were almost washed away. There were warnings about mines in the ground and unexploded bombs. They had to get across rivers where the bridges had been blasted to smithereens, and there were burned-out houses and vehicles everywhere they went.

"If I didn't hate the Germans so much, I'd almost have respect for them," Stanislav said as they drove past the abandoned positions. "Their death warrant's already been signed, but they're still fighting back."

"Who's going to build all of this back up again?" Peter sighed as they drove through yet another field of rubble that used to be a village. Voytek leaned over Peter and stuck his head through the window to watch a horse that was wearily pulling a cart.

On the cart sat a family, with all of the belongings that they'd been able to salvage. Stanislav drove past, blowing his horn, and they laughed and waved. The children pointed excitedly at Voytek. Stanislav stopped and gave some food to the parents.

When he got back into the truck, he said, "As long as

we keep on going forward, we're going to win. And as long as we're winning, we'll keep on going forward."

"What do you mean?" asked Peter.

"That one fine day we're going to chase those Germans all the way back to their own country and that when they're there, we'll put a big fence around it to keep them in, with a dome over the top, and we'll seal it all up so that we'll never have to see them again or smell the stench of sauerkraut for the rest of our lives."

Stanislav took a deep breath and said happily, "Speaking of which, don't you think it smells a bit less like sauerkraut today than it did yesterday?"

Peter shook his head and lit a cigarette. "As far as I'm concerned, this is the only thing that helps," he said and he blew out a big cloud of smoke.

But Stanislav was right. When they returned to the camp that evening, Pavel came running over to their truck. "He's dead!" he shouted. "He's dead! The great leader is dead!"

"What? Who's dead?" Peter shouted through the window.

"Hitler, of course!"

"Holy Mary, Mother of God," Stanislav yelled. He stepped so hard on the brake that Peter and Voytek bumped their heads on the windshield. Stanislav leaped down from the truck and jumped onto Pavel. Then Peter piled on, and Janusz, and Lolek.

Voytek lolloped around the pile of soldiers and finally grabbed the nearest leg, which happened to belong to Pavel. Voytek pulled Pavel out from under the rest and then started tugging on the other legs, until all of the soldiers stopped and pounced on Voytek instead. They carried on romping around until Voytek suddenly shook the soldiers off him. He raised his nose in the air and his nostrils trembled.

"He can smell something," said Lolek.

"Dead sauerkraut," said Stanislav.

"No. Beer," said Janusz. "I just saw them lugging barrels over there."

There was a party mood in the camp and Voytek was about to have the best summer of his life. The soldiers couldn't go home yet, but there was no fighting either. The war was over.

They moved to a new camp, by the sea. Voytek had a bath every day and stuffed himself with pears, apricots, peaches, and apples. Italy was crippled and shot to pieces, but the trees were full of fruit, as though they wanted to say: think of the future, because life will go on.

And when the soldiers apologized for their greedy bear, the farmers all said, "Don't worry about it. Let him enjoy his taste of peace. And take whatever you want for yourselves, too."

It was over a year before the soldiers finally received orders to leave Italy, in the fall of 1946. They couldn't go home yet: the Germans might have left Poland, but the Russians were occupying the country now. Poland still wasn't free.

The Polish soldiers had fought alongside the British, so they were welcome in Scotland. They all climbed back onto a ship, and this time there was no problem about taking the animals.

Voytek even had his own official rations card. It was supposed to last him a week. But he'd raced through his cigarettes in the time it took for them to be handed out,

After liberation

and then he moved right on to the chocolate and the sugar. A couple of hours later, when everything was gone, he went to visit his friends and to see if he could scrounge any more goodies.

"You're getting fat," said Peter. "I'm not giving you anything else."

"When you already weigh about five hundred pounds, what do a few more matter?" said Stanislav, handing Voytek a chocolate bar. And when Stanislav had run out of chocolate and cigarettes too, it was his turn to go begging.

Everyone begged from everyone else until finally there was no candy or cigarettes on the entire ship. They all agreed it was about time they arrived in Scotland.

21

"A bear! A bear!" the children cried from the dockside as Voytek's ship came into port at Glasgow. Voytek stood up at the railing, looking curiously at the big crowd of people standing in the rain and waving at the ship.

When the ship had docked, the soldiers gathered, the Poles with the Poles, the British with the British, and marched down the gangplank. Voytek marched along with them, walking on his back legs.

Everyone crowded around to watch the big brown soldier. And Voytek enjoyed every minute. Anyone would have thought he was the commanding officer and that the men had won the war under his leadership — which was, of course, why the soldiers in his company all had a picture of Voytek on their uniforms.

Voytek would have been happy to carry on marching. The dry land under his feet felt wonderful and the applause and cheers from the crowd were very nice indeed, but it was time for the troops to disband.

The British soldiers were on home soil and they all went their own way. The Polish soldiers had to be patient. They were given a place to stay in a camp on the other side of the country.

Stalin and the dalmatian had already left with the British soldiers by the time Voytek got into the truck with his friends.

"It's better this way," Peter said when they were driving

to their new home. "They wouldn't have understood that they were saying goodbye anyway."

"Goodbye's for humans," Stanislav said. "Animals just leave, without making any fuss, and that's the best way to do it."

The others nodded.

"War's all about goodbyes," said Lolek.

"Hey, Lollie, don't start all that again," said Stanislav. "You'll have us sobbing away like a bunch of girls and it doesn't help one bit."

As the soldiers sat in silence, looking outside and watching the raindrops trickle down the windows, Voytek pressed his nose up against the ventilator. It smelled different here. Curiously, he sniffed the strange scents. It was the smell of Scotland, his new home.

"Hey, come here, old mate," Peter said one afternoon. He had a chain in his hand, with a collar on it. Voytek had raided the kitchen yet again and even though the cook in the new camp had, of course, made friends with him, he asked Peter if there was anything he could do to keep Voytek away from the food.

Peter put the collar around Voytek's neck, but there was no way he could fasten it. "You're not telling me you've put on even more weight, are you?" Peter took a look at the collar and saw there was no room for a new hole.

"Hurry up," Stanislav called from the jeep. "We're already late."

"I know," said Peter, "but I have to get this chain on Voytek."

"Just put the collar on his leg instead."

"Like an elephant?"

"Hey, if it works," said Stanislav. And Peter fastened the collar around one of Voytek's back legs.

"We'll be back soon, greedy-guts," Stanislav called through the window and they raced off with screeching tires.

Voytek sat down and took a good, long look at his leg. He soon started tugging away at the collar.

A crowd of men and women was already sitting and waiting when Peter, Stanislav, Pavel, Janusz, and Lolek came running into the hall. Everyone clapped when they saw them. Peter apologized for their late arrival, but no one was upset. Someone quickly ushered the soldiers to their places in the front row.

"Welcome, ladies and gentlemen," said the chairman of the meeting. "We are here today for a most unusual vote."

"Yes, yes," shouted a few people from the audience.

"Today we are going to vote on a new member." All eyes were on the five soldiers in the front row.

"We members of the Scottish-Polish Society are in agreement that Private Voytek should become a member of our society. However . . ." and here the chairman paused. He reached into the inside pocket of his jacket and held something up. It was the emblem of the transport company of the 2nd Polish Corps.

"How did he get hold of that?" Stanislav whispered.

"Distinguished members," the chairman continued, "this exceptional soldier has achieved something remarkable. Not only did he serve as an ammunition carrier for the Polish army, but more importantly he was a mascot, providing great support for the boys on the front who fought for our freedom." Thunderous applause and cheers came from everyone in the audience.

"What are they planning?" Peter said.

"Which is why, ladies and gentlemen . . ." The chairman's voice faltered and he took a sip of water, "which is why I wish not only to vote on his membership, but would also like to propose that Private Voytek should be made an honorary life member of our organization."

All of the members rose to their feet and cheered and clapped and shouted bravo and the people nearest to the soldiers slapped them on the back.

"Is that a yes?" the chairman shouted above the tumult. He banged his gavel on the lectern until, finally, there was silence.

"I require a show of hands," he said. "Is that a yes?" And every person in that room raised a hand. And there was more clapping and whistling and the crowd sang the Polish national anthem, followed by "God Save the Queen." And then they drank vodka and whiskey and the chairman presented the soldiers with a big pot of honey. "I imagine that this will go down well with Voytek," he said.

"Hmmm," replied Stanislav.

"What do you mean?" asked the chairman.

"Well, actually, he prefers beer," said Peter.

"And cigarettes," said Stanislav.

The chairman raised his eyebrows and went to get some bottles of beer. "I'll just keep the honey for myself, I think," he said with a laugh.

At the end of the afternoon, the jeep with the five soldiers in it swerved a little as it drove back into the army camp. Peter and Stanislav jumped out before Lolek had even parked up properly. They took the bottles of beer from the back seat and ran over to where they'd left Voytek.

"Oh, no!" said Peter. His shoulders slumped and he sobered up immediately. The chain and the collar were lying on the ground, but there was no sign of Voytek.

"The cook's going to kill us," said Peter.

"He's going to kill you, you mean. Not us," said Stanislav. They ran to the kitchen, but Voytek wasn't there.

"Haven't seen him," said the cook, looking very happy. It wasn't long before Voytek came lumbering over. His fur was dripping wet and there was a water lily on his head.

"Oh, dear God," said Peter.

"The neighbor," said Stanislav. As he spoke, the owner of the farm next to the camp came running up, closely followed by the soldier who had been standing guard.

"That bear! He was in my pond," the farmer shouted at the soldiers. "Does he belong to you?"

Voytek sat down and put his paws over his eyes.

Peter apologized and Stanislav started removing the water plants and duckweed from Voytek's fur.

"He made such a splash when he jumped in," the farmer continued. "All of my carp went flying up into the air. It was raining fish!"

Stanislav burst out laughing. He couldn't help himself. "S-sorry," he said through the laughter, "Sorry." And he fell onto his back, roaring with laughter. Everyone else joined in, even the farmer, and Peter handed him a bottle of beer. When Voytek heard the bottle being opened, he took his paws from his eyes and looked to see whether there might be one for him too.

As Voytek was downing his bottle of beer, Peter promised the farmer it would never happen again. "From now on, we'll keep him on the chain."

"You sure about that? asked Stanislav.

"Absolutely certain," Peter replied. The men all looked at one another and smiled.

22

A year after their arrival in Scotland, the soldiers received the news that they could finally go home. Excited men were running all over the camp, but there were five men with worried faces: Peter, Stanislav, Pavel, Janusz, and Lolek.

"He can't come with us," said Lolek.

"He has to," said Peter.

"How do you think your parents will like that?" said Janusz.

"I'll just have to go and live somewhere else, won't I?"

"What will you do with him when you go to work?" said Pavel.

"I'll find a job where he can come along."

"So you'll be working at the zoo?" said Stanislav. "The zoo in Warsaw will be just a heap of rubble. There won't be any jobs for you there."

Peter shrugged. "I'm still taking him with me."

The day of departure was getting closer and the news from Poland wasn't good. The whole country was in chaos. The Germans and the Russians had been on a rampage. Not a single brick or stone was in the same place as before.

"I arranged something with a zoo once before," Lolek gently said to Peter. "Do you think I should give it a try in Scotland?"

"We'll go with you," said Pavel, Janusz, and Stanislav. And Peter finally realized that he had no other option than to follow their advice.

On November 15, 1947, it was time to go. They all climbed up into the truck for one last trip: Peter, Voytek, and Stanislav in the front, Janusz, Pavel, and Lolek in the back. When they reached the zoo in Edinburgh, they found the director waiting for them at the gate.

Voytek climbed down from the truck and looked around, curiously.

"Come with me," said the director. They had made a new home for Voytek next door to the penguins. Trustingly, the bear walked into the enclosure, followed by the soldiers.

They gave Voytek a few affectionate thumps and Peter removed his chain.

"Hey, ammo-carrier," Stanislav said. "You behave yourself, okay?"

On the way back, the men didn't speak for a long time. The wind was whistling so hard through the gaps in the cab that Stanislav couldn't even get his cigarette to light.

"Would you do it for me?" he asked Peter. And when the cigarette was finally lit, Peter said, "We had no choice, did we?"

"No," said Stanislav, "just like we couldn't have left him in that sack five years ago."

And when the day came for all of the soldiers to leave for Poland, Peter, Stanislav, Lolek, Janusz, and Pavel did the same as Stalin and the dalmatian.

They left the way that animals leave. Silently, without making any fuss.

Afterword

Voytek was born in January of 1942 in the mountains of Iran. He died on December 2, 1963, in the Edinburgh Zoo in Scotland.

He served in the Polish army for over five years and spent the rest of his life in a zoo. Peter Prendys had a difficult decision to make. He knew Voytek couldn't go back to Poland with him.

Voytek missed his fellow soldiers very much at first, but he soon became good friends with his keeper. And whenever he heard someone speaking Polish, he pricked up his ears, ran over to the fence, and begged for a cigarette.

Voytek became the most famous bear in the world. He was everyone's favorite at the zoo and journalists came from all over to visit him and write about him. The director of the zoo also used to visit him regularly for chats.

Voytek was a Syrian brown bear. This is a subspecies of the ordinary brown bear, but smaller and blonder. There are only a few of these bears left in the world. But, once in a while, one is sighted in the mountains of Syria, Iran, or Iraq.

If the soldiers hadn't bought Voytek from the little boy,

he'd probably have ended up in the circus. Or he'd have had to learn how to dance on a hot plate with a ring through his nose.

Most of Voytek's friends returned to Poland in 1947, but some of them stayed in Scotland and they often went to visit Voytek at the zoo. They climbed over the fence to play with him. The keepers didn't approve, but Voytek's friends didn't pay any attention to them.

During World War II, Voytek gave the 120 soldiers in his company the courage to go out every day and help to liberate Europe. Not only did he make it easier for the soldiers of the transport company to feel brave and to keep up their courage, but everyone who saw him forgot the misery around them for a moment, whether it was a high-ranking colonel or a ten-year-old Italian boy. He was a friend and a mascot who made the war easier to bear.

And that's how Peter described Voytek, that day at the port in Alexandria, isn't it?

With thanks to:

Soldier Bear by Geoffrey Morgan and W. A. Lasocki
Silent Heroes by Evelyn le Chêne
Europe at War by Norman Davies
The Sikorski Museum in London for the tour and permission to use the photographs.

Voytek with one of the Polish soldiers

Voytek in the truck with his emblem

Kaska and Kubus

Bibi Dumon Tak has written several nonfiction titles for children, beginning with *The Cow Book* in 2001. In her books Bibi blends literary technique with fact to produce stories that are both compelling and accurate. *Soldier Bear* is her first novel based on a historical event. Bibi lives in the Netherlands.

Philip Hopman was born the youngest son of a tulip farmer. But he chose a career in children's books instead of tulips, and he has illustrated more than 150 books since 1988, including *Earth to Stella* (Clarion) and *22 Orphans* (Kane/Miller). Philip also lives in the Netherlands.